THE
COLLECTOR

THE COLLECTOR

*A **MAURO BRUNO** DETECTIVE SERIES THRILLER*

ALAN REFKIN

THE COLLECTOR
A MAURO BRUNO DETECTIVE SERIES THRILLER

iUniverse books may be ordered through booksellers or by contacting:

iUniverse
1663 Liberty Drive
Bloomington, IN 47403
www.iuniverse.com
844-349-9409

ISBN: 978-1-6632-5440-5 (sc)
ISBN: 978-1-6632-5441-2 (e)

Library of Congress Control Number: 2023912926

Print information available on the last page.

iUniverse rev. date: 07/20/2023

To my wife, Kerry
and
Fran and Raylee McGough

I

The frail eighty-three years old Italian man was five feet four inches tall, had gray hair that was sparse in spots, and walked with a cautious gait, keeping his movements slow and his stride short. His name was Dottore Cristoforo Milani, although he was known to employees of the fifty-four Vatican Museums by his descriptive moniker, the curmudgeon, because of his age and gait. Born in Rome to affluent parents who survived World War II with their wealth intact because they'd kept their money in a Swiss bank, he showed an early love of art. He was admitted to the Accademia di San Luca, the second oldest art academy in Europe and the most prestigious in the country, where he gained an encyclopedic knowledge of art, artists, and the painting techniques they employed. After receiving his doctorate in art history and distinguishing himself at smaller museums, he was hired by the Vatican Museums at the age of thirty and became its curator twenty years later, responsible for seventy thousand works of art, twenty thousand of which were on display. The Museums, as with everything in the Vatican, were under the authority of the pope, who delegated their oversight to the secretary general of the Vatican's Governorate. The curator was third in the pecking order. No trustees, governing boards, committees, or other bureaucratic layers existed.

The curmudgeon remained curator for thirty years, leaving in early 2022 when he reached the mandatory retirement age of eighty. Because he was a micromanager and spent all but his sleeping hours at the Museums, he never married, had few friends, and had no hobbies. Retirement bored him. Therefore, because the only thing that made him happy was to be around art, he established a daily routine of going to the Vatican Museums when they opened at eight-thirty and looking at works in the various galleries before having a late lunch at the Bistrot La Pigna in the Courtyard of the Pinecone and returning home. Occasionally, that routine was broken when the pope invited him to his apartment, the two having established a strong friendship over the years. During their talks, the pontiff would inevitably ask the former curator a seemingly endless list of questions about the life and works of his favorite artist, Leonardo da Vinci. Milani, an expert on Renaissance masters and their paintings, had an encyclopedic knowledge of these artists and spoke at length to the pontiff about Il Florentine, which da Vinci was sometimes called in his time because the famed artist and inventor lived near Florence.

The pope's curiosity was because of his birthplace—the two hundred-person hamlet of Anchiano, which was less than forty miles from Florence. Given the size of the hamlet, one might assume that the pontiff was the most famous person to begin their life on that small patch of earth. However, that assumption would be wrong because, in 1452, Leonardo da Vinci took his first breath in Anchiano. That commonality made him feel incredibly connected to the Renaissance master and his works, his favorite painting being the Mona Lisa.

The pope's admiration for da Vinci, and that they were from the same hamlet, resulted in his lobbying the French government for more than a decade to allow the Mona Lisa to be displayed at the Vatican, even though Milani told him there was little chance of this happening because the painting had only left France three times since it was first exhibited in the Grand Gallery of the

Louvre in 1804. Therefore, the pontiff wasn't surprised when each request was politely denied. However, one day a thought came to him when he realized that asking the French to do something extraordinarily rare was fruitless unless he reciprocated by exchanging an equally rare work of art. Subsequently, his next request to the president of France proposed sending da Vinci's Saint Jerome in the Wilderness and Raphael's Transfiguration to the Louvre for two weeks in exchange for exhibiting the Mona Lisa at the Vatican for the same duration. That suggestion came from Milani, who said that Raphel's work would be of particular interest because it was commissioned for the French cathedral at Narbonne by Cardinal Giulio de' Medici, who instead donated it to adorn an alter in Italy, where it has been ever since.

The president of France consulted with the Louvre's curator, asking for his opinion on the exchange. With ten million visitors to the Louvre annually, and eighty percent viewing the Mona Lisa, the curator was reluctant to let the museum's number one exhibit and the most valuable painting in the world leave its protected confines. However, the thought of bringing another da Vinci and Raphael's Transfiguration to temporarily replace it, and the publicity and crowds that would ensue, was irresistible and changed his mind.

Once he recommended to the president of France that they accept the pope's offer, a deal was struck and a date set for one year in the future, which would allow both museums time to put in place the transport and security arrangements for the nearly two billion dollars in paintings that would pass between them.

For those who planned the exchange, the year passed quickly. The day soon arrived when, on a charter flight with heavy security and a police motorcade from the Ciampino Airport, the Mona Lisa made the eleven-mile journey to the Vatican and was taken directly to its exhibition space in the Room of the Creed in the Borgia Apartments, which was on the first floor of the Apostolic Palace.

The Apostolic Palace was the official residence of the pope and contained the papal apartments, various offices of the Catholic Church, public and private chapels, the Vatican Museums, the Vatican Library, the Sistine Chapel, and the Borgia Apartments. However, this pope did not reside there. Instead, wanting to live in less lavish surroundings, he resided in a suite in the Domus Sanctae Marthae, a building adjacent to St. Peter's Basilica, which was used as guest quarters for clergy coming to the Vatican and as the temporary residence for members of the College of Cardinals who took part in the papal conclave to elect a new pope. The Room of the Creed, one of six rooms comprising the Borgia Apartments, displayed frescoes of the Apostle's Creed on scrolls held by the twelve apostles, the creed being Christian teachings.

The Vatican's current curator, who'd held that position for a year, was at the Louvre when the Mona Lisa was taken from the Grand Gallery in its environmentally controlled and bulletproof enclosure, and rode in the back of the armored vehicle transporting it to the Charles de Gaulle Airport, keeping it within eyesight until it arrived at the Room of the Creed.

Inside the Borgia Apartments, six discretely armed men in civilian clothing, formerly with Italy's special forces, supplemented Vatican security. The exhibition area was similarly secure, with everyone entering the Apostolic Palace required to pass through an airport-style security scanner. Within the Room of the Creed, three infrared-capable cameras monitored the painting from different angles, and a ring of floor-to-ceiling laser beams surrounded its environmental enclosure. Breaking a beam produced an audible alarm and activated a lockdown of the Borgia Apartments and Apostolic Palace, sealing entry and exit doors, which now required a code from the pope or Vatican security to reopen. It also meant that the Swiss Guard, armed with automatic weapons, would surround the Apostolic Palace and secure the entry and exit points of Vatican City.

At six pm the day the Mona Lisa arrived, there was an invitation-only viewing. Guests included clergy, politicians, and others who had enough influence with the Vatican to avoid buying a ticket and standing in line. For this special viewing, the laser beams were inactivated to allow these VIPs to stand in front of the protective glass and scrutinize the da Vinci masterpiece. The former curator was one of the invitees.

It took two hours before the crowd had thinned enough for Milani to get a close look at the painting, which he'd viewed several times when visiting the Louvre. After standing for more than twenty minutes with his eyes nearly pressed to the bulletproof glass, he removed the camera from his pocket, accessed the magnifier app, and took a closer look at several sections of the masterpiece. Several minutes later, he returned the phone to his pocket and searched for the person who had replaced him as curator, seeing him speaking with the pope at the far corner of the room.

"What you did was remarkable," the curmudgeon said to the pope, interrupting the conversation.

"Your hard work and diligence made the exchange of paintings with the Louvre a fait de complet by the time you retired."

"I want to talk about that exchange. I'm surprised that the French promised you they'd send the original Mona Lisa and instead provided a replica. I guess they don't trust anyone, even the bishop of Rome, to safeguard it."

"This is not a replica, Cristoforo," the curator interrupted indignantly. "I inspected this masterpiece before it left the Louvre, authenticated it as da Vinci's Mona Lisa, and kept it constantly in sight until it was brought into this room."

"Nevertheless, it's a forgery."

"That's impossible."

"Take a look," he responded, pointing to the painting.

The younger curator believed the curmudgeon had dementia or impaired eyesight. However, noticing the pope's uneasiness because of Milani's accusations, he reluctantly agreed to examine the painting again and followed the former curator to the exhibit.

"This is the original work created by the hand of da Vinci," the younger curator reaffirmed after a five-minute examination.

"Look closely at the face. The subtlety and sfumato are off."

The young curator looked again at the painting. "You're mistaken," he replied.

"Explain subtlety and sfumato," the pope asked the curmudgeon.

"Leonardo used thirty layers of paint to create the subtleness of Lisa Gherardini del Giocondo's expression."

Because of his past discussions with Milani, the pope nodded in understanding that instead of saying the Mona Lisa, the curmudgeon gave the name of the wealthy silk merchant's wife and mother of five, who was the subject of the painting.

"The layers of paint on the original," the curmudgeon continued, "have a known thickness of forty micrometers or half the width of a human hair. This layering is substantially thinner, changing the subtlety by a fraction," Milani replied, taking a dig at the curator.

"And how can anyone discern with the naked eye a variance in the thickness of paint that's less than that of a human hair?" the young curator asked.

"I can. But even if the subtleness was the same thickness, it's nearly impossible to reproduce da Vinci's genius at layering the unique colors he mixed to create the desired effect. The best a forger can hope for is to produce an effect that would be difficult to detect. The better the forger, the greater the difficulty in discerning the variance in subtlety. This forger was excellent."

"And sfumato?" the pope inquired.

"The sfumato was Leonardo's way of softening the transition between colors, allowing the tones and colors to shade gradually into one another. This produced a soft outline."

"The sfumato and subtlety of the painting I just inspected are certifiably by da Vinci's hand," the young curator countered. "None of the art experts in attendance this evening saw the irregularities you claim."

"They would if they took an objective look. I've spent six decades examining Renaissance paintings, and I'm very familiar with the techniques and idiosyncrasies of artists during this period. This is not da Vinci's Mona Lisa. It's a magnificent forgery of that masterpiece."

The young curator was exasperated, his voice displaying his frustration with what he perceived to be the curmudgeon's stubbornness. "Are you implying that the Mona Lisa has been stolen and replaced with a replica?"

"I'm not saying the painting's been stolen, just that the French might not have trusted us with the original."

"And they assumed we didn't have the expertise to detect a forgery? That's preposterous."

"It's an exemplary fake which, from a distance, is impossible to detect," Milani countered. "It fooled you and every other expert in this room."

Knowing that neither person would change their view, the pope intervened. "I'd like to know if the painting on display is the Mona Lisa," he told the young curator. "Can we scientifically determine if it's a replica?" he asked, suggesting a means to settle the dispute between the current and former curator.

"I'll have the chief restorer and his staff return to the Vatican and, when the exhibit ends this evening, have them analyze the painting," the young curator said, knowing he had no choice now that the pope wanted a scientific confirmation.

At ten pm, the VIP exhibition ended. Once the last guest left the Apostolic Palace, the alarm system was deactivated, and the restoration staff brought the Mona Lisa to their laboratory. Once there, the painting was carefully removed from its protective case.

"We'll begin with the X-ray fluorescence spectroscopy, or XRF, to study the paint layers and their chemical composition," the chief restorer told the pope as six of his staff gently carried the painting to the machine.

"What will this tell us?" the pontiff asked.

"The composition of the pigments used by the artist and the number of layers of paint. As a control, I have pigment graphs from one of our da Vinci paintings," the chief restorer said.

The chief restorer aimed the XRFs handheld analyzer at various parts of the painting, the readings transferring to his desktop computer, where a program converted them into a series of blue graphs. He then brought up a series of red graphs from a known da Vinci painting.

"The red graphs are from Saint Jerome, which this lab previously authenticated as a work of da Vinci," the chief restorer stated. "You'll notice thirty red graphs, each corresponding to a layer of paint the artist used to create subtlety. The shape of the graphs shows the chemical analysis of the pigments used in each layer. If the number of graphs and their shapes are the same, the number of layers and the composition of the pigments are identical."

"There are only fifteen blue graphs, and their shapes differ completely from the control readings," the young curator said, his voice showing his surprise at the findings.

"Meaning the Mona Lisa in our possession is a fake," the restorer said.

The young curator collapsed on a nearby chair.

"What should we do?" the pope asked Milani.

"The Mona Lisa is scheduled to be returned to the Louvre in two weeks. We have that long to find out what happened because when we return the painting, the Louvre's curator will look closely at it to ensure its authenticity. If he didn't know he sent a replica, he'd believe we lost the most valuable painting in history. By lost, I mean it was stolen on our watch. However, if he intentionally sent a fake, he'll say everything is fine," Milani stated.

"We can't wait two weeks to see what scenario unfolds because, if it's the first, our failure to return the real Mona Lisa will mean the Vatican will be accused of incompetence, and we'll no longer be trusted to exchange art with other museums. The French may also decide to keep the works of art we sent them until we return da Vinci's masterpiece."

"The unanswerable question seems to be how do we find out if the French didn't trust us with the Mona Lisa or if it was stolen? And, if it's the latter, who took it, and where it was taken? The museum is an assemblage of art historians and administrators, not investigators."

"Any effort at discovering the truth will require your expertise," the pope said. "Without scientific equipment, only your eyes can determine if a painting is an authentic da Vinci or a replication."

"We'll still need someone capable of finding the Mona Lisa."

"I know someone who can send that expertise."

"What does he do?" Milani asked.

"She," the pope corrected, "works for the Italian government, and from my experience, I can unequivocally say that she's the modern-day equivalent of what the Church referred to centuries ago as its head inquisitor."

2

Pia Lamberti was sixty-two years old, five feet six inches tall, and had black hair and soft brown eyes. The widow of the former president of Italy, she was Italy's intelligence czar, a position she requested be a state secret as a condition for accepting the job. Answerable only to the president of Italy, she felt that putting herself on an organizational chart would subject her to the scrutiny of the nine-hundred-and-forty-five members of the Chamber of Deputies and the Senate of the Republic, the legislative branches of the government. It would also invite her decisions to be second-guessed by the President of the Council of Ministers, the Interministerial Committee, and the Department of Information Security—all involved with the country's intelligence apparatus. Therefore, her office was funded by the country's black budget.

She was often referred to as the witch, a moniker attributed to her by one person, but which rapidly spread among her enemies and insiders who knew of her position because the name seemed to suit her belief that most threats were empty promises made by those unwilling or unable to carry out violence. In contrast, she was a proponent of taking action rather than engaging in dialogue and had no compunction about unleashing violence if it suited her purpose. Never showing all her cards or thoroughly reading someone in on her plans, she looked for a person's frailties and exploited them.

The witch worked from her residence, the largest in the Parioli area of Rome, an enclave of mansions on magnificent tree-lined streets just north of the Villa Borghese gardens. The 1930s-era homes were a magnet for the affluent who wanted to live in the city yet be far enough away from business and commercial areas to have their privacy. Lamberti's estate occupied one side of a short residential feeder street. A fifteen-foot-high wall encompassed the five-acre spread, and a similarly high twin wrought-iron gate opened to a gravel driveway that led to the mansion. The witch's office, on the second floor, could have been on the cover of *Architectural Digest*.

Lamberti answered a call from President Orsini at 6:30 am, learning that the pope had just phoned and requested her help on a matter of vital importance to the papacy. An insomniac, the intelligence czar was already at her desk and arrived at the Vatican an hour later with her bodyguard and driver, Franco Zunino. Also serving as her assistant, Zunino was thirty-one years old, six feet two inches tall, had short black hair, and had an athletic build with broad shoulders and a narrow waist.

The Swiss Guard greeted the witch, and with Zunino waiting with the vehicle, escorted her to the Room of the Creed in the Borgia Apartments, where the pope, the curmudgeon, and an athletic-looking man six feet two inches tall with ramrod straight posture and salt and pepper crewcut hair were waiting. Behind them was the Mona Lisa sent by the Louvre, which had been returned to its case and put back on display.

"Forgive the early morning call," the pope began, "but this exhibit opens in an hour, and as you saw, there's an enormous line waiting to see the exhibit." He then introduced Milani and Colonel Andrin Hunkler, the commandant of the Swiss Guard.

Lamberti, not into small talk, asked how the Italian government could serve the papacy, knowing that because the president sent her to provide whatever assistance was needed, she had little choice but to accept the pope's request.

"President Orsini has spoken about you and, although vague on your responsibilities, implied that you were his problem solver."

Lamberti was silent, and her face expressionless.

With the witch not choosing to comment, the pope broke the awkward silence. "The Mona Lisa in front of you is a forgery," he began. "This has put the Vatican in an impossible position. We don't know if the French sent this fake because they didn't trust us with da Vinci's masterpiece or if it was stolen before its arrival. I need you to determine what happened and, if it was stolen, to retrieve the original."

"Is the painting always kept in that enclosure?"

"That's what I'm told."

Lamberti stepped closer to the masterpiece and examined the case. "Removing it from the enclosure appears time-consuming. Was this Mona Lisa inspected before it left the Louvre?" she asked.

"The curator inspected it prior to its departure and kept it within sight until it reached this room. However, his ability to discern an authentic from a forged da Vinci leaves something to be desired," the pope said, telling her how the forgery was discovered.

"Therefore, stealing the painting during transport seems improbable," Lamberti stated.

"I agree. The open question is whether the French government or a thief made the substitution," the pope stated. "I need you to get proof that the Louvre substituted the painting and, if they didn't, to find the Mona Lisa and get it to the Vatican within two weeks, when it's being returned to Paris."

"That may not be possible."

"I know, but from what the president has said, you at least have the tools to conduct this investigation. Without your help, finding the truth would be a hopeless endeavor."

"To be clear, you're asking our government to conduct a clandestine investigation on foreign soil, because this investigation will start in Paris."

The pope, the curmudgeon, and the colonel looked apprehensive, believing that statement meant there was a possibility that Lamberti would decline to get involved because the discovery of their activities would create a diplomatic firestorm for the Italian government.

Lamberti saw their look of concern. "However, because the request for my involvement comes from the president, the Vatican will have my full attention in resolving this matter. Do you know Dante Acardi?" she asked, already knowing that both the pontiff and the colonel were familiar with the former deputy commissioner of the state police.

The pope and Hunkler nodded.

"Three weeks ago, I appointed him to lead the Agenzia Informazioni e Sicurezza Interna, which you may know as the AISI, the national intelligence agency focused on international security. In sensitive situations, he uses a small investigative group not affiliated with the government. I'll appoint him the point person for this investigation."

"I know and trust Dante. Is this investigative group BD&D Investigations in Milan?" Hunkler asked.

"It is."

"The pope and I worked with Mauro Bruno and Elia Donati when they exposed the Bank of Rizzo's embezzlement of money from the Vatican."

"Since then, they've added a partner, Lisette Donais," Lamberti continued.

"When will they start?" Hunkler asked.

"In about ten minutes."

BD&D Investigations previously had two offices, one in Donais' Paris apartment and the other on the second floor of a five-story historic residential building that was steps from Milan's Duomo. However, because she spent most of her time in Italy, Donais vacated the lease on her Paris home and moved to the apartment in Milan, which was both a residence and office. It was twenty-eight hundred square feet and had four bedrooms, the partners using a rectangular conference table in the center of the living room as their communal desk.

Mauro Bruno was a former chief inspector with the Polizia di Stato in Venice. He was fifty-two years old, five feet eleven inches tall, had salt and pepper hair combed straight back, and a neatly trimmed black mustache with intruding flecks of grey. Not comfortable in casual clothing, he usually wore a dark blue suit, white shirt, and light blue tie because his late mother liked the look and said it distinguished him. Elia Donati was forty, six feet tall, and had black hair held in place with enough mousse to keep every hair immovable. He was tan, clean-shaven, and always dressed as if he was going to a GQ magazine photoshoot. Lisette Donais was five feet four inches tall and a doppelgänger for Jennifer Aniston. At thirty-three, she had the torso and legs of a model and a voice that was sensual without being flirty.

The three investigators were sitting at their desk at eight when they received Acardi's call asking them to come to Rome and meet him at Lamberti's residence, adding that they were booked on the eight forty-five flight from the Linate Airport and that the boarding passes had already been texted to their phones.

"Milan traffic is heavy this time of day. We may not make it," Bruno cautioned.

"Lamberti told me the plane won't leave without you," Acardi responded.

Bruno smiled, knowing the immense power she held.

It had been three weeks since they'd last seen Acardi and Lamberti. They'd sat in her second-floor office where the newly appointed head of the AISI offered BD&D a steady stream of business with the caveat that he wanted priority on their time.

Because they'd previously worked with Acardi and respected his judgment, they agreed to his terms after Bruno added they could reject any proposed assignment.

Once the call ended, the investigators quickly packed and took a taxi to the airport that was four miles from downtown, arriving fifteen minutes after the scheduled departure time. Taking Acardi at his word, they walked to the gate, where they found one security guard at the entrance to the jetway and another in front of the open aircraft door. Once the three were onboard, the guard told the pilot he was free to depart and allowed the flight attendant to close the aircraft door.

The plane landed at the Ciampino Airport at ten, after which the three deplaned, made their way through baggage claim, and exited the main terminal. They saw Zunino standing beside Lamberti's second car, a Range Rover Defender, parked at the curb. Twenty-eight minutes later, they arrived at her residence.

The exterior of the three-story, thirteen thousand square feet mansion reflected Lamberti's love of the Italianate style, combining the nineteenth-century phase of classical architecture with stylistic features of the sixteenth-century Renaissance. That meant it had prominently bracketed cornices with a campanile or bell tower at one end and a belvedere or structure meant to take advantage of the view at the other.

Once through the gates, the Rover parked near the front door. A man in a black suit with a matching tie and a white shirt approached the trio, carrying a scanning wand in his right hand. After they were wanded and patted down, Zunino escorted them past the guard with an AR-15 assault rifle, standing to the left of the front door.

"We went through airport security. Why are we being searched, Franco?" Bruno questioned as they followed him into the residence.

"Signora Lamberti doesn't want to interfere with her security team's routine. If she makes an exception, she believes the guards may become uncertain about whom to search or watch. Rigid security procedures are critical for her safety."

The three investigators couldn't disagree with that philosophy and followed their escort up the staircase to a set of double doors. The guard standing in front of them followed their movements and stepped aside as Zunino approached. As they entered the room that served as Lamberti's office, they saw her seated in a club chair at the head of two facing sofas with an antique coffee table in between. Acardi was on the couch to her left.

Lamberti was stylishly dressed in a dark business suit, a white silk blouse, and Valentino pointed-toe pumps. Adorning her neck was a Mikimoto Reserve Akoya pearl necklace. She directed the trio to the couch across from Acardi.

"I have an assignment which I'd like you to accept," she said, after recounting her conversation with President Orsini and the pope.

The three investigators appreciated Lamberti's habit of getting straight to the point without social banter.

"We find the Mona Lisa, whether in the Louvre or in the hands of whoever stole it," Donais summarized.

"That's your assignment."

The three investigators looked at one another and nodded, agreeing they were up for the challenge.

"Where will you start?" Acardi asked.

"I assume in Paris," Lamberti said.

"That's where the mystery began," Bruno stated. "I'd like to get a feel for the Louvre's security and see the room in which the Mona Lisa was exhibited. Switching a painting in that environment would be a highly complex endeavor requiring an insider's knowledge. Therefore, it would be easy for the Louvre to replace the masterpiece with a fake and keep that substitution secret to all but a few."

"Since none of you can detect the Mona Lisa from a paint-by-numbers version of the masterpiece, I'm having the former curator of the Vatican Museums, Cristoforo Milani, accompany you. With half a century of experience, he'll be able to discern the original," Lamberti said, handing Bruno an opaque one-inch by three-inch envelope and explaining what was inside.

The three investigators and the Milani arrived at Orly Airport at three that afternoon and took a taxi to the Hotel Regina on the Rue de Rivoli and across the street from the Louvre. They were booked into the three-bedroom Parisian Suite. Donais and Milani had separate rooms, while Bruno and Donati got the room with two beds. Once settled, they decided to go across the street and see the Salle des États, the room where the Mona Lisa had been displayed, where the two paintings on loan from the Vatican were being exhibited.

"The Museum is open until six; that gives us almost two hours," Milani volunteered.

"Let's get moving," Bruno said.

The four walked across the street but found the line to get inside so long that it was apparent they wouldn't have much time inside. Bruno was looking at his phone to see if the museum offered VIP tickets when Milani told the investigators to follow him. Walking to the security guard at the entrance and speaking to him in French, he gave him a card identifying him as the Vatican Museums' Curator Emeritus.

"I want to see your exhibition of my paintings," he explained.

The guard went to his supervisor, who took Milan's request up their chain of authority until it reached the curator. Believing that someone on his side screwed up and didn't tell him that a group from the Vatican Museums was coming to visit, he rushed outside, greeted the four, and gave each a full-access pass attached to a lanyard.

"No one told me you were coming," the curator apologized.

"Bureaucrats," Milani responded with a shrug, drawing a laugh and a nod from the curator.

The two curators, who'd never met, seemed to strike it off and, oblivious to the investigator's presence, carried on a conversation as they wove through the museum, eventually entering the Salle des États, the largest room in the Louvre. On display were the two Vatican masterpieces. Just as with the Mona Lisa, the closest anyone could get to the paintings was fifteen feet, with the velvet-roped perimeter and two security guards enforcing that distance.

The investigators looked around the room and saw a security camera facing each Vatican painting, assuming they'd been re-tasked from monitoring the Mona Lisa. As they evaluated the room's security, Milani pulled aside the velvet rope and approached the paintings. The Louvre's curator waved off the guards who moved to stop him and joined the curmudgeon, who spent ten minutes looking closely at the da Vinci and Raphael masterpieces.

"I never tire of seeing such beauty," he told the other curator. "The Louvre has a reputation for having the finest masterpiece restoration department in Europe. Would it be possible to see it while I'm here?" the Milani asked. "In return, I would insist that you let me reciprocate by giving you a private tour of the Vatican's treasures and restoration areas. As you know, some items have never been displayed and have only been seen by past curators and popes."

Hearing this, the Louvre's curator would have given Milani a key to the museum's front door if he'd asked. "This way," the curator said, briskly leading the way.

The museum employed nearly one hundred restorers, conservators, conservation scientists, and conservation preparators assigned to independent departments based on the composition of what was to be examined. These included objects, defined as three-dimensional works of art; paintings; works on paper; photographs; and textiles. Milani was taken to a paintings workspace where a Renaissance-era masterpiece was being restored.

As they entered the room, the investigators saw two cameras on a central pivot. Looking at the direction they were pointed, and assuming each had a wide-angle lens, their field of view blanketed the restoration area but ignored the alcove containing a row of supply cabinets and a small bathroom, which, because of their position, would have required a third monitoring camera.

While the investigators combed the room, the two curators spoke to the chief restorer, who was inspecting a Caravaggio, a Renaissance painter known for his intense realism and strong contrasts. Milani's friendly banter discovered that he'd only recently been promoted to his position after his predecessor retired.

With nothing further to see, the four left the museum at six and returned to their hotel, Milani remaining strangely silent until they entered their room. During their walk, it was hard to ignore that his jaw was clenched, brows furrowed, and his skin had reddened—signs that he was highly irritated.

"What's wrong?" Bruno asked.

"The scope of your investigation is going to expand considerably because the two Vatican paintings I sent here have been replaced with forgeries."

"What?" Bruno exclaimed, his partners also expressing a look of disbelief.

"I spent a lifetime with those masterpieces. It's as if I've lost two family members," he said, upset at what he'd discovered.

"Someone at the Louvre should have detected they were forgeries. You did," Donati said.

"Detection is a matter of suspicion and confidence. There was no suspicion because they came from the Vatican Museums. There was confidence because they believed our staff of experts authenticated them."

"Which explains why the Louvre's curator didn't notice the forgeries," Donati said.

"There was a presumption of authenticity, just as with the Mona Lisa," Donais added.

"Exactly. It's another matter when a masterpiece is being sold. Provenance is verified and goes through a battery of scientific tests, including the age and composition of the canvas or wood and an analysis of the paint pigments. Some paintings are also known to have part of another painting beneath them, the artist abandoning his initial work in favor of the one we see. X-rays expose these. The list goes on. However, these methods are seldom employed when there's no change in provenance or a question of authenticity. At a museum, the replacement of an original work with a forgery is discovered during the periodic inspection of a painting to determine if it requires restoration. That's when an expert looks at it closely."

"If the curator of the Vatican failed to detect the fake Mona Lisa, and the Louvre's curator similarly didn't detect the two fakes on display, whoever painted them must have extraordinary skills. The list of these individuals can't be long," Bruno said.

"I know of seven who have the requisite skills, but there are likely others whose names haven't been exposed."

"How long does it take to replicate a masterpiece?"

"That depends on the artist, each of whom employs different techniques, the complexity of the painting, and the intricacies required to replicate the appearance of age. Wolfgang Beltracchi, whose fake appeared on the cover of a Christie's auction catalog, is rumored to have forged around thirteen hundred paintings. Pei-Shen Qian sold one of his forgeries for eighty million dollars. He's replicated dozens of masterpieces."

"Faking the age of a painting must be difficult."

"It requires a detailed knowledge of the materials an artist used, where and when the art was painted, and the techniques employed by them. Take, for example, the cracking on a painting. Eighteenth-century French paintings tend to crack like spider webs. In Flemish works, the cracks resemble tree bark. In Italian Renaissance paintings, they'll look like untidy rows of brickwork.

The cracking I observed on the three fakes was extremely good and in line with what one might expect from a period piece."

"Getting back to why we're here," Bruno segued, "does anyone believe the three masterpieces are hidden in the Louvre and that the curator knowingly sent the forged Mona Lisa to the Vatican?"

"Based on the thefts of the Vatican paintings, I'd say he's in the dark," Donais stated. "Which leads to the questions of how they're substituting the real paintings for the fakes given the constant surveillance we witnessed, and removing them from the museum, since the thief obviously can't walk the paintings past security."

"It could only happen in the restoration area," Milani said, "where a masterpiece is removed from its environmental container so it can be inspected."

"That makes sense," Donais stated, her partners agreeing. "From what we observed, the restoration area has two security cameras. If we could get ahold of those feeds, depending on whether they still have them, we can see if that's where the switch was made. However, I don't know how to obtain the recordings without the curator asking why we need them."

"We don't need to ask him. We need to ask Montanari," Bruno said.

"Montanari?" Milani questioned.

"Indro Montanari is a reformed thief and genius tech wizard," Bruno stated as he attempted to phone the savant, but the call went unanswered.

"Didn't he tell you to delete his number from your phone?" Donati asked with a smirk.

"I'll be the first to admit that our work history has had a few holes in the road."

"More like crevices."

"Nevertheless, if we're going to look at the recordings, we need his expertise," Bruno stated.

"Stepping out on a ledge," Donati said, "you might consider that he's not answering because every time you call or go to his home, you're asking him to do something illegal, and he doesn't want to go back to jail."

Donati's exchange with Bruno was like a soap opera to Milani, who sat on the couch and was glued to their conversation.

"His unique skills are often the only way we can get to the truth," Bruno admitted.

"Any idea on how to get him to answer your calls?" Donati asked.

"One, and he won't like it."

Indro Montanari was thirty-seven years old, five feet six inches tall, had black hair that he kept short enough so that he didn't have to comb it, and weighed one hundred thirty pounds, which was anorexic by Italian standards for a person his age. His daily uniform was Levi jeans, a loose-fitting, long-sleeved black uncollared shirt, athletic shoes, and rectangular-shaped black Balenciaga glasses. The ex-thief became wealthy hacking computer networks and, with a superior knowledge of electrical engineering, bypassing sophisticated electronic entry systems that were marketed as impossible to penetrate. His life of crime ended when Bruno, then a chief inspector in the Polizia di Stato, apprehended him during a robbery when Montanari touched the wrong contact on a cipher lock circuit board and set off a silent alarm, the break-in getting him a five-year sentence. Two years into that term, Bruno needed help to bypass an RFID system securing the vault at a home he had broken into. Calling him in prison, he asked for advice on how to get past the vault's security system. Montanari couldn't believe that the person who arrested him was asking for help to commit the same crime that sent him to jail. Nevertheless, he told Bruno how to get past the embedded security protocols, enabling the chief inspector to open the vault and expose the person who killed his father. In gratitude, the chief inspector arranged for the last three years of the savant's sentence to be commuted and set him up as a security consultant in Rome, getting him the Vatican as his first client. Once it was discovered that the Vatican used his services, he had no trouble attracting clients.

Bruno and Montanari were friends, but that relationship was tested over the years when he asked the savant to occasionally perform illegal activities, although the results saved lives and put bad guys, who'd committed crimes far worse than thievery, in prison.

The savant was in the kitchen stirring a pot of spaghetti sauce which, along with cannoli and red bull, was his kryptonite. He made a fresh batch weekly and was at the end of the sauce's four-hour simmer. He'd just torn a hunk of ciabatta bread, which had much larger holes within the dough than traditional bread, making it perfect for dunking, and was about to dip it in the sauce when he heard a knock at his door. Setting the bread aside and walking to the door, he looked through the peephole and saw a five-foot, six-inch tall woman dressed in an elegant, dark business suit with a white blouse. Behind her was a six feet two inches tall athletic-looking man. Having previously worked with Lamberti on another of Bruno's escapades and knowing Zunino, he opened the door and let them enter.

"This is for you," she began, handing him a box of cannoli. "Mauro Bruno sends his regards and wonders why you're not answering his calls."

"You know why," he said.

"I do, but he's at an impasse without your help. That's why I'm here." She walked past him and sat in a chair, gesturing for him to sit on the couch beside her.

Knowing that refusing her request wasn't an option, he sat down as Zunino closed the front door and stood in front of it.

"I want to employ your services again," she said.

Those words sent a shiver through the savant because he knew the matter wasn't up for discussion, and he didn't want to get involved with anything that was cloak and dagger, the only area in which Lamberti operated. The last time he tried to refuse her offer of employment, she told him that she'd put him in jail for the rest of his life for the dozens of transgressions he committed that went unpunished. "If you think there's going to be a trial in open court, you're wrong," he recalled her saying. "The proceeding will be private and in front of a very unsympathetic three-judge panel. I hope this clarifies that requesting your services was my way of being polite."

"And if I perform and forget about these services?" he'd asked.

"I'm your protector."

This time, avoiding the inevitable restatement of those threats, he asked what Bruno wanted.

"First, a little background," she said, explaining that the Mona Lisa sent to the Vatican was a forgery and that two paintings loaned to the Louvre had also gone missing and were replaced with fakes. "Bruno needs your help to find them. Give me your phone."

The savant complied. Lamberti dialed Bruno's number and handed him the phone.

3

Montanari began his attack on the Louvre's computer system following a conversation with Bruno and Milani. In his experience, the easiest way of penetrating an organization's database was to find which part of that business allowed outsiders to communicate with it. For a business, this usually meant the human resources department, which routinely posted job openings and accepted responses and resumes from applicants.

The savant did a Google search, found the link advertising job openings within the museum, and attached a virus to the email he sent to the contact person at human resources. Although the Louvre had firewalls, sophisticated anti-virus, malware, and other software customized to keep people like Montanari out, his algorithm evaded detection by hiding as a benign part of a legitimate file. Once inside the Louvre's computer system, the virus attached itself to the human resources person's computer access privileges, allowing Montanari to enter the museum's intranet.

Two hours after he inserted the virus and used a companion program to translate from French to Italian so that he could easily navigate within the computer system, he called Bruno and asked for the specifics of what he needed.

"I need access to the archives for the museum's security cameras so that I can view the recordings. Can that be done?"

"I'll make it happen," the savant confidently responded. "However, security feeds aren't usually kept for long. If nothing happens within a defined period, they're recorded over."

"Find out how long they keep their recordings," Bruno said, ending the call.

Montanari picked up a cannoli, took a bite, and followed that with a gulp of Red Bull. Although he was in the museum's system, that didn't mean the human resources person he was impersonating had access to the security camera feeds. Moments later, the savant discovered they didn't and needed another of his hacking tools to attach the virus to a person in authority who had that authorization. Looking through the museum's email directory, he found the digital address for the curator, who he assumed would have access to the camera system monitoring his paintings. That assumption was correct, and after a brief look at the archives, he phoned Bruno back.

"The Louvre doesn't erase its recordings," the savant said. "They keep an archival file for every security camera. Since digital storage is cheap, I'm assuming they're either extraordinarily cautious or they deem the recordings historical footage that can be seen by future generations. Either way, the security cameras mean they aren't likely to replicate the previous theft of the Mona Lisa that went unreported for some time."

"It was stolen before?" Donati asked.

"In 1911," Milani interjected, "by three Italian handymen who spent the night in the art-supply closet and, in the morning, lifted the two-hundred-pound protective glass case containing the painting off the wall, removed the wooden canvas, wrapped it in a blanket, left the museum, and took a train out of the city. No one noticed the painting was missing for twenty-eight hours until a still-life artist set up his easel in the gallery, saw it was missing, and decided he couldn't paint without it being there."

"That's when they noticed the painting was missing?" Donais asked.

"Unbelievably, no. Since the cameras of the day didn't take indoor pictures with any degree of quality, it was common to bring works of art to the roof to be photographed. When the still-life artist asked a guard to see how long the photographers would have the Mona Lisa, the guard went to the roof to check, returning to say they didn't have it. Twenty-eight months later, the Mona Lisa was recovered when one of the thieves tried selling it to an art dealer in Florence."

"An Einstein moment," Donati commented.

"Since the Louvre keeps every camera feed," Donais said, "we can look at previous feeds from the Salle des États and see when the switch occurred."

"Hopefully," Bruno added, saying they weren't dealing with amateurs and, if the museum made the switch, the last thing they'd want was for posterity to know what they did.

"Let's start with the Mona Lisa's removal from the Salle des États for its trip to the Vatican and go backward in time from there. Can you do that and show us the feed on your screen?" he asked Montanari.

"Absolutely, but if the museum staff didn't make the switch, and the painting was stolen some time ago, it'll take an inordinate number of hours to examine the feeds. I'll write a program to detect when the Mona Lisa was moved, and it'll jump to each of those moments."

"How long will it take to write that program?" Bruno asked.

"Around thirty minutes to write it. After that, I estimate twenty to thirty minutes to link the camera feeds and approximately an hour to wash them through the program. These times are guesstimates, at best. It could take much longer because I'll be working inside the Louvre's system and need to be cautious so I don't trigger a hacking alarm, which will lock me out."

"Do it," Bruno said.

"Forty-five minutes later, the savant sent Bruno a link to sync their computer screen with his.

The program noted several times in the past three years, the timeframe Montanari selected, when the masterpiece was moved from the Salle des États. The three investigators and Milani began with the most recent movement, which showed the environmental enclosure, with the Mona Lisa inside, being taken off display for its journey to the Vatican Museums, the pope's curator's eyes locked on the painting as it left its exhibition space.

"Let's see the previous movement," Bruno said.

That occurred three months earlier when the Mona Lisa was taken to the museum's restoration facility, everyone following the journey on successive camera feeds, which Montanari accessed. The masterpiece was gently removed from its case and inspected by two people who examined the painting with headband magnifying glasses, similar to those used by physicians and dentists. The case was taken from the room during the examination and returned thirty minutes later.

"Explain why these people are examining the Mona Lisa and where the protective case went," Donati asked Milani.

"It's nothing unusual. Museum paintings are frequently inspected by outside restoration experts to determine if any portion requires repair," Milani said. "The frequency of the inspections and what painting is scheduled are at the curator's discretion. I suspect the Mona Lisa would be looked at once a year. At the same time, the temperature and humidity controls within its protective case would be checked by engineering for wear and parts replaced if necessary. Annual inspections were requisite for top-tier Vatican masterpieces when I was curator."

"Why outside experts?" Donati persisted.

"The reasons vary. Sometimes it's because the experts have more knowledge than the restoration staff about the type of painting being examined. Other times it's because the museum wants another set of eyes to examine it to avoid complacency by the museum staff."

"Let's look at the prior movement," Bruno said to Montanari. That occurred a year earlier, and just as before, the painting was removed from the Salle des États and taken to the restoration facility where the same two individuals inspected it. Afterward, the Mona Lisa was returned to its protective case and brought back to its exhibition space. "Did you notice anything different between this inspection and the one three months ago?" Bruno asked.

Donati and Donais said they didn't. Milani said it was the crate.

"Go back to the inspection that occurred three months ago," Bruno told Montanari.

The savant did.

"Stop the recording when I tell you," Bruno said as he looked intently at the feed. "Now. Look behind the museum employee," he told Donati and Donais.

"Workbenches, chairs, and a large rectangular wooden crate or container on a four-wheel dolly that has Louvre Abu Dhabi stenciled across it," Donais said.

"I was too focused on the painting to notice the crate," Donati admitted.

"There's a Louvre in Abu Dhabi?" Donais asked.

"It's a ninety-two thousand square feet museum in the United Arab Emirates and the sister museum to the Louvre Paris. It opened six years ago. The Emirati licensed the Louvre's name for thirty years and established an exchange program with this museum," Milani interjected.

"That explains some of what I saw. Let's see if there's a crate in the background the prior year," Bruno said. "Can we do that, Indro?"

Montanari did.

"There's no container," Donati and Donais said, both using crate and container interchangeably as they watched the feed until the Mona Lisa was returned to the Salle des États.

"Did anyone notice that, in this feed, the Mona Lisa was returned to its exhibition space much sooner than in the last?" Bruno asked.

Everyone acknowledged they did.

"Indro, can we compare the times?" he asked.

The savant said he could, leaving the conversation and returning to say that it took thirty minutes longer to return the Mona Lisa to the Salle des États three months ago than it did a year earlier."

"Let's have another look at those clips," Donais said to the savant, who again queued it for them.

"In both inspections, the two experts leave once they're done, presumably not wanting to wait while the Mona Lisa is returned to its protective case and brought back to the Salle des États," Donais said.

"I assume the person wearing the white lab coat and standing beside the experts is the museum's restoration specialist," Bruno stated.

Everyone agreed with that assumption.

"And he's alone with what we now believe to be the original Mona Lisa," Donati said.

As they continued to look at the feed, they saw the person they assumed to be the restoration specialist push the container off-camera and into the alcove where the file cabinets and bathroom were located. Moments later, he carried the Mona Lisa into the same area, returning with da Vinci's masterpiece after several minutes.

"What was that about?" Donais asked.

"When I first saw this, I assumed he had to go to a bathroom and didn't want to take his eyes off the Mona Lisa. But now, I'm not so sure," Bruno said.

The others said they had the same belief.

"As a hypothetical," Donati intervened, "since the two experts have just verified the original, there's an assumption when the Mona Lisa is returned for display that it's the original painting. What if the fake was inside the Abu Dhabi container, and instead of going to the bathroom, our lab-coated person exchanged it for the original? He had the perfect cover knowing when the experts would be there and that they leave before the painting was returned to its protective case."

"How long was it between the time the museums agreed to exchange masterpieces until they went on exhibition?" Bruno asked Milani.

"A year."

"That's more than enough time to schedule the thefts around the expert's annual inspection and have one or more master forger paint three replicas," Bruno said.

"And, since no one can get within fifteen feet of the painting while it's on display," Donati added, "everyone believes they're seeing the original."

"And the Vatican paintings were stolen in the same manner," Donais volunteered.

"That would be my guess. Let's look," Bruno said.

Montanari got the feed for the day the two Vatican paintings arrived. The restoration room camera feeds showed that the Vatican's paintings were moved off-camera before being brought back into view several minutes later and returned to their protective cases.

"This means the real Mona Lisa, and possibly the Vatican's paintings, because we didn't see the containers in which they were placed, are being shipped to an unknown destination, which we assume is the Louvre Abu Dhabi, but can't confirm because we didn't see the shipping label," Bruno summarized.

Everyone agreed with that assumption.

"Can you get the name and background of the person in the lab coat who we think is the restorer?" Donati asked Montanari. "We need to have a chat with him."

"Let me look."

"His name is Preuet Dages." Montanari answered ten minutes later. "He quit the day after the Mona Lisa was sent to the Vatican. The bad news is that a Google search of his name brought up an article in *Le Parisien*, Paris' daily newspaper, saying he died in a hit-and-run traffic accident that same day."

"Mio Dio," Milani said, meaning dear God.

"That was convenient. What now?" Donais asked.

"We determine if that container went to the Louvre Abu Dhabi and, if not, where it was sent," Bruno stated.

"I may be able to help," Montanari stated, saying he could access the Louvre's shipping and receiving department and would see if they had a record of shipments to the sister museum. He later returned to the conversation to say that Museum Shipping, an art transport company, picked up three crates, preferring to use that term instead of container because they were constructed of wood, the following morning. "All were sent to the Louvre Abu Dhabi," he said.

"Do we know if they were delivered to the museum?" Donati asked.

"The records only show they went to the Charles de Gaulle Airport and were placed on a nonstop flight to the Abu Dhabi International Airport where, two hours after the plane landed, receipt was acknowledged by Museum Shipping at the customs warehouse. That's where the shipment record ends."

"Is Museum Shipping based in Paris?" Donais asked, hoping they could find out more by visiting the company.

"It's a UAE company based in Abu Dhabi."

"Can we hack into their computers to determine if the museum received these shipments?" Bruno asked, hopeful that Montanari could get them that information.

"Let me see," he said, everyone in the room listening to the clattering of his keyboard until he returned to the call.

"Not this time. Their website doesn't list an email address; therefore, I can't introduce a virus into their system. It only allows someone to fill in their name and phone number with the promise of a return call. That's smart."

Although it was getting close to midnight, the savant was energized by the twelve-ounce cans of Red Bull that he'd been steadily drinking, each containing one hundred eleven mg of caffeine. In comparison, twelve ounces of Coca-Cola Classic contained thirty-four.

"Does it say who owns Museum Shipping?" Bruno asked.

"Let me take a closer look at the information bar on their website and do a Google search," the savant said, coming back with the name Sheik Walid Al Nahyan. "He's the leader of one of the UAE's six royal families, on the board of the Louvre Abu Dhabi, and according to *Forbes*, has a net worth of fifty billion dollars."

"The shipping company's earnings have to be a financial gnat to someone with his wealth," Donais volunteered. "He may not know much, if anything, about this company's operation or even who runs it for him."

"Since we believe the shipping company's containers are how the fake paintings were brought into the Louvre and the originals smuggled out, and know that the containers left Paris and arrived in Abu Dhabi, we need to take a close look at the company," Bruno said.

"By taking a close look, you mean searching the company for the paintings?" Donais asked.

"That's exactly what I mean. If the paintings aren't at their facility, we may be able to find where they were taken. In any event, it's our only lead," Bruno said, with Donati and Donais agreeing that searching Museum Shipping was a necessity.

"Are you up for a flight to Abu Dhabi?" Bruno asked Milani.

"I'll go anywhere if it will help find the stolen paintings."

"Thanks, Indro; I'll get back to you," Bruno said, ending their call.

"Do we need a visa to visit the UAE?" Donais asked.

Donati accessed Google on his cellphone and learned that Italian citizens could obtain a visa upon entry.

"There's an Etihad flight leaving for Abu Dhabi in a few hours," Bruno said, looking at flights on Expedia. "The flight duration is seven hours and, with UAE time three hours ahead of Paris, we leave at 6:00 am Abu Dhabi time and arrive at 1:00 pm. I'll need you to pay for this until we get reimbursed," he said to Donati, who came from a wealthy family but, instead of following his father into a lucrative business career, became a police officer in the Polizia di Stato because of the satisfaction it gave him to help those who were unable to help themselves.

"I'll book the tickets," he said without hesitation. "Business or economy class?"

"Lamberti won't have an issue with business class. She'll want us rested when we get there. We'll also need hotel reservations. They may not issue us a visa without them."

"I'll find a place," Donati answered and, after purchasing the airline tickets, booked a four-bedroom suite at the St. Regis Hotel on Saadiyat Island.

As Donati was making their travel arrangements, Bruno updated Acardi.

"Is it always this chaotic when you're working a case?" Milani asked Bruno when he finished his call.

"No, this is going much smoother than normal."

4

Dante Acardi was in his early sixties, five feet eight inches tall, of medium build, had short gray hair parted to the right, light brown eyes, and a baritone voice. It was two in the morning when he entered Lamberti's second-floor office to brief her on what he'd learned from Bruno. He'd tried to update her by phone, but she insisted that he come to her office to discuss the situation in person.

"They've made remarkable progress," Acardi said after briefing her on what Bruno said and Montanari discovered. "When will you tell the pope about the missing Vatican paintings?"

"Later this morning. There's no point in waking him. Getting back to Bruno and his team, once they go to the shipping company, they'll have tipped their hand to the sheik. They're in his backyard. After that, if their suspicions are correct about his involvement, they'll be closely watched, making their investigation infinitely more difficult."

From experience, Acardi knew better than to interrupt Lamberti when she was thinking out loud.

"They'll need someone to cover their backs," Lamberti said. "Colonel Hunkler?"

"That's what I was thinking. They could use his expertise, and he doesn't have a connection to our government."

"Bruno will like that since he and Donati have previously worked with him. I'll tell Bruno."

"No. I don't want him or the others to know. If Hunkler joins the team, we're just adding another log to the fire and giving the sheik someone else to watch."

Lamberti went to her computer, learning that the next flight to Abu Dhabi was an Etihad Airline flight from Fiumicino Airport that left in ninety minutes. She booked Hunkler and told Acardi to tell him he was on it and to brief him on what was happening on his way to the airport.

"Tell him to look at his phone. I'll have texted his boarding pass, hotel reservation, and car rental information by the time he reaches the airport."

"He doesn't work for us. He's the commandant of the Swiss Guard and reports to the pope," Acardi reminded her, knowing that technicality wouldn't deter Lamberti.

"That's my problem, not his. I'll phone the pope later," she answered, ending the discussion.

Hunkler listened to what Acardi told him. Knowing the pontiff had requested Lamberti's assistance, he expected the pope to go along with whatever she wanted. He hurriedly packed and left for the airport ten minutes after receiving the call, arriving at the departure gate twenty minutes before the doors closed. As a precaution, Lamberti had called the airport's night manager and instructed them not to let the Etihad flight leave the gate until he was onboard. Although the manager didn't know her position within the government, all it took was a statement that she worked for President Orsini to make her request an edict.

Abu Dhabi, the capital of the United Arab Emirates or UAE, is on a small triangular island of the same name and is connected to the mainland by a short bridge. In Arabic, "Abu" means father, and "Dhabi" means gazelle. Subsequently, Abu Dhabi means father of the gazelle, the name believed to have originated because of folk tales that spoke of gazelles on the island.

Hunkler's Etihad flight landed at 12:30 pm, twenty minutes before Bruno and his team. He obtained his visa, cleared customs and immigration, and went to the Hertz rental counter on the fourth level of the Sky Park Plaza outside terminal one, where he was handed the keys to the white Toyota Land Cruiser that Lamberti rented for him. The drive to the Saadiyat Rotana Resort took fifty-five minutes in traffic, his hotel four miles from the St. Regis, where the investigators and Milani would be staying. After checking into his room, he drove there, parked across the street, and waited for Bruno to arrive.

Bruno's flight was similarly uneventful and landed ten minutes early. After everyone got their visas and cleared customs and immigration, they took a taxi to their hotel, arriving at 2:10 pm. On their way, Bruno called Acardi.

The five-star hotel, comprising fifty floors in two buildings, was on The Corniche, a stretch of beach with restaurants, biking corridors, and walking paths. Having been served two meals on the plane, no one was hungry, and they were eager to get started. The warehouse was eight miles from the hotel and close to the Louvre Abu Dhabi. After leaving their bags in their suite on the twentieth floor of the first tower, they returned to the lobby, where the concierge arranged for a car and driver to take them wherever they wanted. Minutes later, they got into a white GMC Yukon XL Denali, which was for the exclusive use of hotel guests for a price, and left the St. Regis.

Traffic was generally bad in Abu Dhabi, and although they were only going eight miles, the streets were congested, and it took twenty minutes to get to Museum Shipping. Pulling into the lot after them was a white Toyota Land Cruiser, which parked thirty yards away.

The fifty thousand square feet warehouse was kept at forty-five percent humidity and at a temperature of sixty-five degrees Fahrenheit, which contrasted sharply with the ninety-seven-degree furnace and fifty-five percent humidity outside. However, because the Emiratis considered this temperature to be frigid, every employee inside wore a jacket.

Although it wasn't planned, and ignorance is sometimes bliss, the four arrived slightly before three—the time for Asr, when employees gathered for twenty minutes of prayer. Subsequently, no one was at the receptionist's desk. Entering the building unseen, they decided to look around and see what they could find until someone questioned what they were doing in the warehouse.

Because the value of the paintings and antiquities the company transported could be hundreds of millions of dollars, no insurance company would issue a policy protecting against theft or damage unless the shipping company had a secure area to keep the art while it awaited pickup or shipment. Therefore, the four focused on finding this area, believing that was where they'd find the stolen art and that they'd improvise how to get inside once they saw it.

As they started down the hallway on the other side of the receptionist's desk, they heard the chanting of prayers. Walking further, they passed an open doorway on their left, which led to a large room where a dozen employees knelt on prayer rugs in a sujud or prostration position. Careful not to make any noise, they continued down the hall, which ended in a large concrete-floored room. To their left were rows of art containers. To the right was an office, with a Dell laptop and DYMO label maker on the desk and a massive vault at the rear.

"I think we found what we're looking for," Bruno said as they entered the office and approached the vault.

"We'll have to ask Lamberti if she has any ideas on how to get into this bad boy without destroying half the building," Donati said.

Knowing they were running on borrowed time, Bruno took several photos of the vault door and said it was time to leave and that they'd return when they figured out how to get into the vault. Milani, who didn't appear to be listening, was instead staring at the vault door and its keypad. As Bruno started to leave the office, followed by Donati and Donais, he grabbed the vault's wheel and pulled. The perfectly balanced door silently opened. Bruno, Donati, and Donais stared in amazement.

Bruno asked how Milani knew it was open, the curmudgeon answering by pointing to the green LED indicator light on the keypad.

"This manufacturer is widely used by the art and antiquity community because their vaults maintain a stable temperature and humidity environment within," Milani said. "A red light on the keypad shows that the vault door is locked, and a green light means it's open. Because the procedures to enter this manufacturer's vaults require two combinations, it's not uncommon for employees to leave it unlocked if they frequently go in and out of it. The Vatican Museums have three such vaults."

As Milani spoke to Bruno, Donati and Donais were mesmerized by the ten paintings inside, none being the Vatican paintings or the Mona Lisa. Milani recognized each and, entering the vault, looked closely at them while Donati and Donais followed and began snapping photos with their cellphone cameras. Bruno was the last to enter and picked up each painting, appearing to examine them closely.

"Are these authentic?" Bruno asked Milani when he finished looking at the last painting.

"Yes, without a doubt, these are original masterpieces."

"I think it's time we leave before we're noticed," Donati interrupted, receiving a nod of agreement from the others.

After closing the vault door, and as they started for the entrance, the chanting that permeated the warehouse suddenly stopped, and they increased their pace toward the lobby. However, just as they came down the hallway, the receptionist almost collided with them as she left the prayer room.

"Can I help you?" she asked in broken English, knowing from their clothing and facial features they weren't of Arab descent and that speaking Arabic would be a waste of time.

Milani thought quickly and removed a business card from his wallet. He presented it to her, explaining in English that they were here because the Vatican wanted to inquire about their services after learning that the Louvre Paris trusted them with their works of art. It was a good comeback, and the receptionist could only respond that management wasn't currently at the warehouse but would contact him. "The four of you are here to inquire about our services?" she asked skeptically.

"And to see the Louvre Abu Dhabi. Please have someone call me," Milani concluded, afterward leading the others through the lobby and outside into the baking sun.

"That was very good," Bruno said as they walked toward the GMC.

"As the Americans would say: when life gives you lemons, make lemonade."

The four returned to their hotel and began looking at the photos that Donati and Donais had taken. "The Portrait of a Woman and Salvator Mundi, both by Leonardo da Vinci; Self-portrait by Vincent Van Gogh; Napoleon Crossing the Alps by Jacques-Louis David; The Subjugated Reader by René Magritte; and The Saint-Lazare Station by Claude Monet," Milani said as they scrolled through the pictures.

"I take it these are well-known works of art," Donati said.

"Some of the most famous, and they have one thing in common," Milani answered.

"Which is?"

"The originals are reputedly on display at the Louvre Abu Dhabi, either as a permanent exhibit or on loan."

"From what we've seen, because of the visual and physical security, it seems impossible to steal these paintings without an accomplice within the museum—someone who knows the system and can make the substitution without being noticed," Donais said.

"The logical assumption being that it's someone in the restoration department," Donati added.

"It would almost have to be," Milani agreed. "That gives us the mechanism for how the thefts are accomplished."

"But we can't confirm that the sheik is the final destination for every stolen painting, including the Vatican's masterpieces and the Mona Lisa. We'll know that when the ten paintings leave the vault," Bruno stated, explaining that Lamberti gave him a packet of GPS microchips smaller than his thumb. "I put one on the underside of each frame."

"You weren't looking at the paintings; you were planting the chips," Donais stated.

Bruno said he was the polar opposite of an art critic.

"How are they attached?" Donati asked.

"Each has an adhesive strip backing. Once I peeled off the protective paper covers, they stuck to the frames like glue. Although their signals won't penetrate the walls of a vault or other metal enclosure, once the chip is out of that environment, it'll automatically connect with a cellular tower or a communications satellite and give the painting's location. Lamberti gave me the GPS chips so she could track us and whoever or whatever we wanted to follow, which includes stolen art."

"Can we track the chips?" Donati asked.

"Only Lamberti. We don't have the necessary equipment because there wasn't time to get it to us."

"She's a smart lady."

"And, as usual, a step ahead of us."

"Do you believe the sheik is behind these thefts? Is he the collector?" Donais asked.

"The collector. I like that moniker," Bruno stated. "He's the front runner. It isn't easy to believe an operation this sophisticated could happen on his turf and be facilitated by a business he owns without him being the beneficiary of those actions. As I said, we'll know more when we trace the GPS chips."

As they continued their discussion, Milani's phone rang. The call was brief, with the octogenarian agreeing with the person on the other end of the conversation. "Sheik Walid Al Nahyan's assistant says he wants to meet with us," he stated to everyone's astonishment once the call ended.

"Why?" Donati asked.

"Why doesn't matter. Given my discussion with the receptionist at the warehouse, we can't refuse."

"Does he want to meet with you or the four of us?" Bruno inquired.

"The assistant emphasized the invitation extended to the four of us."

"Not wanting to repeat what's been said, but doesn't it seem curious that someone with his wealth wants to talk about a shipping contract? My experience with people of serious wealth is that they let others handle the details while they set the objectives," Donati, who came from a very wealthy family and had interacted with his father's billionaire friends, stated.

"It's not about the contract. He wants to find out why we're here and what we were doing in his warehouse," Bruno answered.

"Do you think there was a camera in the vault and that he saw you attach the GPS chips to the paintings?" Donais asked. "That could be the reason for this meeting."

"It's hard to tell. I had to remove the adhesive from each chip before pressing it to the frame. Because the painting was in front of me, the only way someone could see what I did was from a camera behind me. I didn't see one, but that doesn't mean it wasn't there. When does the sheik want to meet?" Bruno segued.

"His driver is on their way to the hotel," Milani said.

The sheik lived on the ninety-second floor of the city's tallest building, the twelve hundred fifty feet high Burj Mohammed Bin Rashid Tower in the World Trade Center complex, five and a half miles from the hotel. Although the sheik frequently conducted business at home, his staff and principal office were on the sixtieth floor of the adjoining building, the Trust Tower.

Upon entering the residential tower, the four were directed to the information desk. Building security was tight, and after their names were verified to be on the guest access log and their passports inspected, each went through airport-style security, their personal items placed in a bin and scanned while they walked through a metal and explosive detection machine.

"No calls or photos are allowed within His Highness's residence," the security guard said, confiscating everyone's phone. "I also need your cellphone numbers for reference," he said, each reciting it as the guard recorded them on a sheet of paper attached to a clipboard.

"We'll return these when you leave," he said. Afterward, they followed him to one of the thirteen high-speed elevators, where he pressed his keycard against a reader, pressed the button for the penthouse, and stepped away. The doors closed, and their elevator ascended at twenty-three feet per second for their ride to the top of the building.

The sheik's one hundred forty-seven thousand square feet residence encompassed the entire floor. Three security guards, one of whom was a female, met them when the elevator doors opened and, after quickly frisking the four and finding only personal items, directed each to remove their shoes and handed them slippers. They were then escorted inside, where Sheik *Walid* Al Nahyan sat on an oversized ornate throne chair raised on a six-inch-high platform.

The sheik was five feet six inches tall, weighed one hundred sixty pounds, and wore a long robe, called a kandura, a ghutra or headscarf, and an agal or rope-like band which held the headscarf in place. All were white. Standing to his right was his bodyguard, Khalil Nedal. He was six feet four inches tall with the physique of a bodybuilder, had a black beard of medium length, and also wore a white kandura and ghutra, but with a black agal. To the sheik's left was a petite woman in glasses. She wore dark blue slacks with a matching blazer and a white blouse.

With a dour expression, Walid Al Nahyan remained seated as Nedal pointed Milani and Donais to the couch on his right and Bruno and Donati to the one on his left. That the sheik didn't stand, talk, or offer refreshments gave the investigators the impression that he believed they were inconsequential.

The petite woman broke the silence by introducing herself in Italian, saying she was one of the sheik's assistants and fluent in over a dozen languages.

"His Highness Sheik Walid Al Nahyan wishes you to know that he will have someone from his company contact you regarding a shipping contract with the Vatican Museums."

"Would it be possible to meet with them tomorrow at the shipping company's office and get a tour of the facility while we're there?" Milani asked, trying to take advantage of the situation.

Instead of asking the sheik, the petite woman posed the question to Nedal, the protocol being that not everyone addressed Al Nahyan, and it was up to him to decide with whom he wanted to converse.

The sheik directed a lengthy response to his bodyguard, who passed it onto the petite woman.

"His Highness said the meeting will occur at four tomorrow, following afternoon prayer. Additionally, His Highness would like you to immerse yourselves in the culture and history of Abu Dhabi and has arranged for you to experience a camel ride through the desert. A car will be at your hotel at eight tomorrow morning, allowing you to complete your ride before it becomes hot."

Bruno, believing that hot was a relative term because breathing the outside air was like sucking in the heat from a stove, told the petite woman to thank the sheik.

Once the woman relayed what Bruno said, Al Nahyan got up without further comment and stepped off the platform, followed by Nedal and the petite woman. As they left, the security guards ushered the four to the elevator. In the lobby, they went to the information desk and retrieved their phones.

The four didn't speak in the vehicle on their way to the hotel, not knowing if the driver understood Italian or if there was a recording device in the car. Neither they nor the driver noticed the Toyota Land Cruiser that trailed fifty yards behind.

As the four stepped off the elevator and entered the lobby, the petite woman returned to her workspace while Nedal followed Al Nahyan to his residential office—a three thousand square feet room decorated with antique Louis XV furniture, the desk at the far end of the office and chair behind it sitting atop another six-inch-high platform.

The sheik went to his desk and, replaying the video on the screen, watched for a third time the security footage of the four entering his vault and taking photos of the masterpieces.

"Inactivate their cellphones and tell the hotel that I don't want them to have access to an outside line. No one can know about what they saw."

"I'll have Etisalat and Emirates Integrated block their incoming and outgoing calls. I'll also have the hotel inactivate their ability to access an outside line and restrict them from the business center. What about the photos on their cellphones?"

"You can erase those photos tomorrow. Once they're dead, ensure access is restored. I don't want anyone to suspect their deaths were anything but an accident."

"Planning ahead, let's assume the GPS chips lead us to the sheik's residence, indicating that the Mona Lisa and Vatican paintings would likely also be there. Any suggestions on what we do next?" Bruno asked, throwing out the question as they sat in the living room and discussed their visit.

"Even if we present them with the GPS tracking evidence and photos, I don't believe the Abu Dhabi police are going to burst into the residence of the head of a royal family," Donati stated.

"That's a certainty," Bruno agreed. "We aren't going to involve the police because it wouldn't do any good and would publicize our involvement. We've committed multiple crimes to get photos of the stolen paintings, and there's no way to prove those paintings were the originals and not copies, which are legal to possess. The sheik can accuse us of extortion or another crime he conjures to discredit us, and any court in this country will accept it with neither Lamberti nor Acardi able to come to our defense."

"It's difficult to understand why someone with his wealth would steal the Mona Lisa or any other famous painting, especially since he couldn't display it. Al Nahyan is a billionaire. He can buy any art that's being auctioned," Donais stated.

"At his level of wealth, you become accustomed to having everything you want," Donati said. "For some, it's about obtaining what no one can buy, even if you're the only one who could see it. That exclusivity is an aphrodisiac for those accustomed to always getting what they want. I know. I've seen it all my life."

"Do you think other members of the royal family are involved?" Donais asked Bruno.

"That remains to be seen. However, everything we've uncovered points to Sheik Al Nahyan as the enabler of the thefts and the probable final destination for the stolen paintings. We're assuming he wants to keep the paintings in the vault and hasn't yet brought them to where he keeps his collection. But what if he's only the conduit, and someone else is the recipient of these masterpieces and the person we call the collector?"

"Why would he be a middleman?" Donais asked.

"Why would a multi-billionaire risk his reputation and standing within the royal family to steal a painting?" Donati also questioned. "Yet, because of his shipping company, we know he's involved."

"Those are good questions. So far, there's only conjecture tying together the snippets of information we've uncovered, and we can be sure there's a multitude of facts we haven't yet found. Although the sheik is the most likely suspect, everything we have on him being the recipient of the stolen paintings, which includes the Mona Lisa, is circumstantial. Yes, he facilitates their theft, but let's not make him the collector by default," Bruno said. "We have one shot at this; if we jump to the wrong conclusion and get off track, we won't have time to correct that mistake and re-focus."

"Do you believe he's the collector?" Donais asked Bruno.

"He seems to be, from what we learned in the short time we've been investigating. If he's not, I think he knows the identity of the person who has the Mona Lisa and the Vatican's paintings. The GPS chips may give us that identity, but investigatively speaking, we're at the tip of the iceberg, and as you know, most of that ice is out of view. Making a definitive judgment this early is akin to ready, fire, aim—meaning we'll miss our target."

"What now?" Milani asked.

"All we can do is wait and see where the GPS chips lead us. The vault is likely a transitory location for stolen paintings, meaning that eventually, the paintings we saw will be delivered to the collector, and that's how we'll find the Mona Lisa. I'll update Acardi and ask him to have Lamberti track the chips," Bruno responded as he removed the phone from his pocket. However, unable to make the call, he looked at his phone and saw no signal.

The others also looked at their phones and saw they had the same problem. Since all used Telecom Italia, they believed they had a common connectivity issue and that the service disruption was only temporary because Bruno had used his phone to call Acardi after they landed. Donati tried the landline in their suite, discovering access to an outside line was unavailable.

"I'll try later," Bruno said. "We might not be able to get a signal in this part of the hotel, and who knows what the problem is with our room phone. I only know that I'm too tired to wait for a technician to troubleshoot the line and get it working. That could take hours. I'll call Acardi in the morning."

5

The sheik's nine-passenger SUV arrived at precisely eight, the petite woman getting out of the back of the extended-length Range Rover and greeting the four while Nedal remained in the front passenger seat. The four wore sunglasses and were dressed in long pants, long-sleeved shirts, and bucket hats. In their hands, they each carried a backpack containing half a dozen bottles of water, aspirin, SPF 50 sunscreen, and lip balm—the result of blitzing the hotel's sundry shop when it opened. Still unable to reach Acardi, Bruno decided to call him when they returned to their hotel, knowing there wasn't enough time to provide an update and answer questions because of their morning schedule. If he still didn't have a signal, the plan was to purchase everyone a burner phone, and Bruno would have Acardi and his tech wizards figure out why they lost reception. He likewise wasn't worried about tracking the GPS chips, knowing that Lamberti was a Type A person on steroids, and had confidence she'd been monitoring them from the moment he landed in Abu Dhabi.

The SUV left the hotel and entered the light, early-morning traffic of the Al Maqta area. Twenty minutes later, the city's towers were silhouettes on the horizon as buildings rapidly faded from view, replaced by the Al Khatim desert on both sides of the four-lane strip of asphalt. They followed the highway for another twenty minutes until the driver slowed and veered onto the hard-packed sands paralleling the asphalt, stopping behind a large open-bed truck with five camels tied to the rear bumper. Standing beside the vehicle was a man in his mid-thirties, who was presumably their tour guide. He was of medium height and weight and wore a kandura and a headscarf held in place by an agal.

As they exited the Rover, the guide approached Nedal, the two conversing for approximately a minute before he joined the four and the petite woman.

"Your tour will last two hours, and we'll return here," the guide said in broken English. "What's in your backpacks?" he said, noticing that each carried one.

Bruno said it was mainly bottled water.

"Give the backpacks to me, and I'll secure them to the saddle posts. Otherwise, it will be difficult for you to get into the bag because of the swaying motion of a camel."

They removed their backpacks and handed them to him.

The guide untied a camel and approached Milani. After getting it into a sitting position and securing his backpack to the saddle post, he explained the basics of mounting and riding the animal.

"Don't look it in the eyes," he began. "Come toward it at an angle without stopping or hesitating. Place your left foot in the stirrup and swing your right leg over the saddle. Once balanced, lean back because a camel stands by extending its back legs first. When you feel this, lean forward while it extends its front legs," he said to Milani, but loud enough so that the others could hear his instructions.

Following what he'd been told, the curmudgeon mounted his ride without issue. Donais, Donati, and Bruno followed without difficulty, with their backpacks secured to their saddle.

"Don't try to control the camel. They can be temperamental and will only listen to their master, which is me. If you tug or pull, it'll get unhappy and may try to bite your leg or throw you off. The more relaxed you are and the looser your grip, the calmer it'll be. Because they sway, let your body go with the motion and swing back and forth with it, holding the saddle post for support."

The guide mounted his ride and came alongside the four. "Camel riding is uncomfortable for those with limited riding experience, and your tailbone will hurt. If you want to take some of the pressure off it, cross your legs up on the saddle to distribute your weight better," he said, demonstrating the movement.

They took his advice and crossed their legs.

Seeing the four were as prepared as they would be, the guide told them to hold on and authoritatively said, "hut, hut, hut." His camel took off at a fast-paced trot, with the others following it single file into the desert.

"Why did he take so much time instructing them if he's going to abandon the foreigners in the desert?" the petite woman asked Nedal as she got inside the Range Rover.

"If they don't have a basic understanding of how to ride a camel, it would take them too long to get deep enough into the desert so they wouldn't have a chance to walk back to this highway."

"We could have killed them and buried the bodies."

"Since we've met with the foreigners, the sheik wants to avoid any hint of foul play and a subsequent investigation by the Italians. Their deaths must appear to be an accident."

"Understood," the woman replied.

"Tribesmen will find their bodies and bring them to the city where the coroner will accurately determine that they died of heatstroke. If the Italians conduct an autopsy, they'll arrive at the same conclusion. The guide's story will be that the group stopped for a rest and, one at a time, he got three of the camels to sit and helped the riders dismount. He was getting the last camel down when the old man tried to keep his beast from turning its head and biting him by pulling hard on the reins and kicking its sides. Instead of sitting, it took off at nearly thirty mph into the desert. After telling the others to stay where they were until he returned, the guide gave chase but lost the old man's trail in the strong morning winds. When he returned to where he left the others, they were gone, his belief being that they also went to look for their companion."

"And the discovery of the corpses?"

"Before he takes his camels and leaves, the guide will text the tribesman the foreigners' last known position. They won't have walked far."

"As usual, you resolved a problem very efficiently," the woman said, complimenting Nedal, who she knew was a narcissist.

"It's easy to kill foreigners in the desert," he said with a note of satisfaction as the Range Rover returned to the highway and headed back to Abu Dhabi.

However, as he would discover, not everything goes according to plan.

When Colonel Andrin Hunkler, who followed the Range Rover from the St. Regis, saw it park near the guide's truck, he pulled off the highway before being seen. Although the areas on both sides of him were desert, they were dotted at intervals with dense stands of rimth shrubs and ghada trees, and he was able to hide his Toyota Land Cruiser behind one so that he could observe what was happening without being noticed.

Seeing five camels tied to the rear of the truck, Hunkler believed Bruno and his team were going for a camel ride and that the Range Rover, which had just left, would return to pick them up at its conclusion. Looking online, he saw the average desert ride was one hour, with one competitor offering a three-hour desert experience. Therefore, knowing he was in for a wait, he reclined his seat slightly, got as comfortable as possible, and waited for their return. Three hours later, with no sign of the

Range Rover or the camels, he called Acardi to see if he'd heard from Bruno or those with him, figuring they might have ended their ride at another spot along the highway and that the Rover met them there.

"Not since yesterday when they were on their way from the airport to their hotel," Acardi responded. "I tried calling their cellphones last night but couldn't get through and didn't have any luck in my three attempts to their room, the hotel operator telling me each time that their line was busy."

"Abu Dhabi's cellphone connectivity puts Rome's service providers to shame," Hunkler said. "I'm on a desert road in the middle of nowhere and have five bars. If I don't have a carrier disruption, how could all four of their devices have zero connectivity in the middle of the city? I'm also not buying their room phone was in constant use. A better explanation is that someone in authority ordered the city's two carriers to block their numbers and had the hotel disable incoming and outgoing calls."

"Which means they've been exposed, creating an entirely different situation and putting them in danger. Where are you?" Acardi asked.

Hunkler gave his GPS coordinates.

"Let me try to get a fix on the GPS chips in their cellphones," Acardi said, bringing up a government tracking program on his computer. "They're stationary nine miles northeast of you," he said less than a minute later, giving Hunkler their coordinates.

"I need a weapon."

"In the UAE, only citizens are licensed to carry them. If you're caught with one, the police won't politely ask how you got it. Instead, they'll throw you in jail and extract that information from you in whatever manner they want."

"Got it. Hold on. Their guide is returning to his truck with four riderless camels in tow and tying them to the rear of his vehicle. This doesn't look good. He and I are going to chat,"

Hunkler said, ending the call as he drove from his hiding place and parked beside the truck.

The guide's expression of puzzlement as to why a vehicle parked beside him on this open stretch of highway turned to fear when he saw that the person getting out of the car had similar facial features to the foreigners he'd just abandoned. That fear ratcheted to panic when Hunkler grabbed his kandura with both hands and slammed him hard against the truck.

"Who hired you to take the four tourists into the desert and abandon them?" he yelled in broken English, his face only inches away from the guide, who mimicked that he didn't understand a word that was said.

Hunkler, who wasn't known for his patience, grabbed the man's throat in an ironlike grip and twisted his head toward one of the camels, pointing to the backpack secured to the saddle post. When the guide shrugged his shoulders, Hunkler decided to elevate his questioning to the next level and punched him in the face, sending the man flying to the ground with a badly broken nose. With blood dripping over his mouth, the guide got up, removed an eight-inch dagger from a long pocket of his kandura, and made rapid slashing movements as he approached the colonel, the confidence in his face believing the unarmed foreigner was no match for his skills.

As he tried to back the colonel into the truck so he couldn't escape, Hunkler stepped forward and deftly brought his left elbow and forearm down hard on his attacker's right arm while shoving his right hand into the man's throat. The simultaneous blows caused the guide to drop the dagger and fall to his knees, gasping for breath.

"Do you speak English?" Hunkler asked as he picked up the weapon and held it to the man's throat.

Still gasping for breath, he nodded that he did.

"I'm going to ask my question again, and if I don't get an answer, I'm going to remove what's important to you," he said, touching his boot to the man's groin.

The guide got the point and told him it was Nedal.

"Are you supposed to call him after you abandoned them?"

"I already have," he answered, taking the phone from a pocket on the opposite side of his kandura from where he removed the dagger.

Hunkler took the phone and tossed it in the back of the man's truck.

"Get the backpacks off the camels," he said.

As the guide started removing them, the colonel looked to see what was inside before putting them in the backseat of his car. Afterward, he cut two strips of material from the man's kandura, bound his hands behind his back, and put him in the passenger seat before tying his ankles.

"Are you going to kill me?" the guide asked.

"If I were going to do that, I'd have already sliced your throat. I have something else in mind. We're going to find my friends, and I'm bringing you along so you don't call Nedal."

"I'd never tell him. I swear."

"Right." Hunkler called Acardi to get an update on the GPS coordinates for the four and, learning they were on the move, put their new location into his cellphone before entering the desert.

It took half an hour for the Toyota to get to the GPS coordinates Acardi provided, where he watched the four climbing a dune in the distance, guessing they were trying to get an elevated view of the area to spot a road or another sign of civilization so they'd know which direction to walk. As his vehicle approached, they waved frantically, having no idea that he was the driver until stepping out of the car.

"Having a bad day?" the colonel asked as the group approached the vehicle.

"It could have gone better," Bruno answered with a smile.

"How long have you been following us?" he asked as Hunkler took bottles of water from the backpacks and handed them to the thirsty group.

"Since you landed in Abu Dhabi. I saw this dirtbag," he said, pointing to the guide in the front seat, "take you into the desert and return with your camels and backpacks. Acardi got the GPS coordinates from your cellphones."

"What are you planning to do with him?" Donati asked, the four looking at the bloodied face of their guide through the vehicle's window.

"I'm going to keep him from telling anyone you're alive until we're out of the desert and ready with our next move," Hunkler said, taking the dagger from the backseat of the vehicle and cutting the ties binding the guides legs before pulling him out of his seat and onto the desert floor.

"How are you going to do that?" Milani asked.

"He had no trouble finding the highway after abandoning you. I'm certain he knows the desert like the back of his hand and can navigate by the stars or sun. I'm leaving him a couple of backpacks with bottled water. That should enable him to return to his truck and reach the highway. If not, I won't feel bad about someone who cold-bloodedly tried to kill you suffering the fate he wanted for the four of you. I have the AC in the vehicle on full. Get in while I cut his hand restraints."

The guide, understanding the situation when the colonel threw the backpacks at his feet, didn't protest. He was confident in the desert and happy to be alive.

Hunkler got into the vehicle, looked at his phone to set a course that would take him to the GPS coordinates he'd recorded before entering the desert, and drove away.

Donais asked how far they were from the highway.

"Thirty minutes."

"What about the camels?" she asked.

"They can go without water for some time. I'll tell the concierge at my hotel that we saw them tied to an abandoned truck on the highway so he can call camel rescue or whatever agency is responsible for animal rescue. If the asshole who tried to kill us makes it out of the desert, he can hitch a ride to the city from one of the vehicles passing along the highway or get back in his truck if it hasn't been towed or stolen. The keys are still in it. Any idea why the sheik tried to kill you?" Hunkler asked Bruno.

"The only reason I can think of is that the inside of the vault had cameras, and he saw we photographed the paintings."

"What vault? What paintings?"

Bruno forgot that he hadn't updated Acardi, which meant Hunkler was also in the dark. He brought him up to speed.

"If I had to guess, I'd say the guide won't get to his truck until tomorrow morning, at the earliest, meaning the sheik won't know we're alive until then," the colonel stated. "If we had any common sense, we'd leave the country before then."

"We can't until we determine if the Mona Lisa's here. If it is, we're not leaving with it and the Vatican paintings," Bruno replied.

"That necessitates that you live long enough to track the GPS chips," Hunkler told him. "If the guide survives and tells the sheik you're alive, Abu Dhabi will be as friendly to you four as Mogadishu was for the Blackhawks."

"For the five of us," Bruno corrected, "because the sheik will find out we have an accomplice. With his resources and a description of you and this vehicle, it won't take him long to discover your identity and put a target on your back."

"What are you going to do while waiting for the GPS data, other than hiding from the sheik?"

"I need to take another look at the shipping company," Bruno remarked.

"Why go back there?" Donati questioned. "We searched the entire warehouse and found the safe."

"We're not going inside the warehouse; we're surveilling it and hedging our bets."

"What does that mean?" Hunkler asked. Donati, Donais, and Milani also wondered, but the colonel beat them to the question.

"It means if the paintings remain in the vault and we don't have a GPS signal to track, we grab and question one or more of the employees to find out where the paintings are taken once they're removed from the vault. We could have done this before, but it would have put a neon sign on our investigation," Bruno said.

"That's a good thought," Donati admitted.

"Can you rent another vehicle?" Bruno asked Hunkler. "I'd like us to have yours."

"I can do that. We'll stop by the airport on our way back, and I'll rent one from a different agency. Do I meet you at the warehouse or the hotel?"

"We're supposed to be dead, so we're not returning to the St. Regis. We'll stake out the warehouse," Bruno said.

"You need to get cleaned up first. You four look like vagrants and are going to attract attention. After I rent another car at the airport, we'll buy you clothes and personal items on the way back to my hotel, where you can shower.

"Good idea," Bruno said.

After Hunkler rented another vehicle, they found a shopping center, bought new threads, including casual wear and business attire, and followed the colonel to his hotel to get cleaned up. As they drove, Bruno revisited an earlier idea.

"Do you remember when you said that whoever was stealing these masterpieces and replacing them with forgeries would need to maintain them, meaning they'd need periodic inspections by an expert and, at some point, some degree of restoration?" Bruno asked Milani.

"I remember."

"If the paintings never leave the vault, and the employees are in the dark where they're taken because the sheik has Nedal or someone else transport them to wherever he keeps his stolen masterpieces, we need another way to find the collector, whether that person is Sheik Walid Al Nahyan or someone else. Therefore, we should start looking for restoration experts who've left major museums and now work for private individuals or have gone off the grid."

"That's good thinking," Milani conceded, "but it will take some time."

"I have a friend who's very good at writing search programs," Bruno said.

"Why do you keep calling him your friend?" Donati asked, knowing that he was referring to Montanari. "He doesn't take your calls and doesn't get involved with us unless Lamberti strong-arms him into helping."

"Perhaps someone I know would be a better descriptive," Bruno told Milani.

6

Once Acardi, the head of Italy's domestic intelligence agency, was updated by Hunkler, he went to see Lamberti. Sitting beside her in the kitchen, each sipped a cup of espresso as he detailed what the colonel had said and discussed how they could help Bruno and his team.

"There are still no signals from the GPS chips I gave him," Lamberti said, Bruno's presumption that she was monitoring the chip's transmissions being correct.

"There won't be any if the paintings are still in a vault."

"Or if the chips have been discovered and destroyed," she countered, revealing her predilection for considering the worst outcome. "If you were the sheik, and a group went unannounced into the warehouse where you hide stolen masterpieces, would you keep the paintings there or move them? His past actions have been meticulous and cautious, demonstrated by the fact that so many masterpieces have been stolen and replaced by forgeries without anyone's knowledge. The thief, whether or not it's the sheik, which is still an open question, doesn't take risks," Lamberti said.

"Let's assume it is Sheik Al Nahyan. As a member of the royal family, what risks does he have? No one will raid the warehouse, search his residence, or open a container, crate, or box with his name on it. We know the paintings will eventually leave the vault because it's a transitory storage area. The question is whether they'll go to the same place where the Mona Lisa was taken," Acardi said.

"Judging by what's happened, we need to give Hunkler and Bruno's team more support."

"The embassy?" Acardi asked.

"That's what I was thinking. Call Hunkler and tell him to stop there on his way to the warehouse. I'll have the president send a message to the ambassador authorizing the colonel to get whatever non-lethal support he needs from their inventory."

"The ambassador won't like being kept in the dark about our operatives in the UAE, especially if their actions could result in casualties or property damage."

"I don't care. A member of the UAE's royal family facilitated the theft of the Vatican paintings, if not outright stole them, and made the pope liable for the disappearance of the Mona Lisa. We're not going to get the paintings back through diplomacy, and Hunkler and the three investigators with him are the bulls in the china shop that I need to make it happen."

Montanari was finishing a program for one of his clients when he saw "no caller ID" appear on his cellphone screen. Ignoring it as a solicitation call, he refocused on programming only to receive a text from Bruno moments later, telling him that he was using someone else's phone and to answer the call. The savant would also have liked to erase the text and turn off his phone, but suspected that the investigator's relationship with Lamberti would mean she and Zunino would pay him a visit if he continued ignoring Bruno. Believing he had no other option, he answered the call that came seconds later.

"What do you want?" he began, venting his irritation at having been interrupted from his work and Bruno's anticipated request for help.

"Your research expertise," Bruno began, knowing that beating around the bush and being social before getting to the point would only irritate Montanari. "I need to know the names and current locations of Renaissance restoration specialists who've left a major museum in the past two years, have not gone to another museum, are unemployed, or have moved to another country, city, or town and are doing the same work for an individual or gallery."

"Have you any idea how much work that will entail? If a museum doesn't publish the restorer's name and area of expertise online, I'll need to hack thousands of museum databases to get their personnel files."

"I'm only looking at major European museums."

"Hold on?" the savant said, returning after a Google search to tell Bruno that Europe had fifteen thousand museums and that he'd need better search perimeters.

"Look at museums like the Louvre, the National Gallery in London, and the Galleria Borghese in Rome because the person we're searching for will be an expert in restoring and maintaining Renaissance masterpieces at upper-tier museums. I know this is a pain in the ass for you, Indro, and you'll have to bend, if not break, a few laws to get me this data. I don't expect you to do this for free. Send me the bill for your time, and I'll make sure that either Acardi or Lamberti pay it. If they don't, I'll write you a check myself."

"Donati has all the money. You're poor," the savant replied with a smile. "Give me till morning."

Hunkler arrived at the warehouse ninety minutes after Bruno and his team, driving a white all-wheel drive Kia Seltos, an SUV that tore up the highway with its ability to accelerate from zero to sixty in nine seconds. He distributed the food, water, binoculars, and burner phones he'd received from the embassy. He kept the Taser for himself because there was only one.

The five split into two groups, the colonel covering the front entrance from the south, hiding behind the dense brush which, although some distance from the warehouse, made him difficult to detect in the fading light of sunset. Bruno and the others would stake out the rear of the structure, taking cover behind an area of tall shrubs that, while hiding most of the vehicle, left a small portion of the roof exposed.

At seven that evening, fifteen minutes before sunset, a large group of employees left the warehouse and locked the front door. Once they departed, three vehicles remained in the parking lot— one of them an extended-length Range Rover which looked identical to the one which brought the four into the desert.

Bruno, Donati, and Donais were prostrate on the ground watching the back of the building through their binoculars while Milani remained in the air-conditioned vehicle. Although they couldn't see the front parking lot, the warehouse blocking that view because of their position, they saw the departing cars and assumed the building would be empty five minutes after the last left. The deep voice behind them evaporated that belief moments later.

"The sheik would like a word with you," Nedal said, surprising the investigators as he and the three thugs who'd accompanied him, each carrying silenced handguns, approached from behind. "Raise your arms and stand."

They did. Looking at his vehicle when he stood, Bruno saw Milani standing beside it with his upper arm gripped by another of Nedal's thugs.

The four were frisked, their burner and personal phones thrown on the ground where Nedal methodically crushed each beneath the heel of his sandal.

"Where is the person who rescued you earlier today?" Nedal demanded.

"I don't know," Bruno answered without hesitation as he looked defiantly at the bodybuilder.

That remark and attitude drew a punch to the stomach so hard the private investigator flew backward and landed on the ground, after which two men roughly pulled him onto his feet and shoved him toward the bodybuilder.

"Where are they?" Nedal again asked.

Bruno gave the same defiant look and answer, which produced the same result.

"You'll be more cooperative when the sheik questions you. Take them to the warehouse," Nedal commanded, giving a hand signal to the thug with Milani to follow.

Hunkler's location gave him a view of the building entrance and where Bruno, Donati, and Donais were positioned. Therefore, looking through his binoculars in the dimming light, he saw their encounter with Nedal and that the four were being taken single file toward the rear of the warehouse. Leaving his hiding place and using the brush for cover, he double-timed toward the back of the warehouse.

He believed that Bruno and the others would already be dead if someone, who he presumed was the sheik, didn't want to question them. That he'd eventually kill them was a foregone conclusion, as evidenced by their encounter in the desert. Therefore, he had a short time to rescue them, although he had no idea how given that he had a dagger and a Taser while those guarding the four appeared to have automatic rifles.

It took five minutes to reposition himself to a spot where he could see the rear of the warehouse. Lying prostrate, and with five minutes until sunset, he watched the four and their thug escorts slowly approach the perimeter-lit building. Looking through his binoculars, he couldn't see any surveillance cameras, which meant nothing because, at this distance, they could be virtually invisible. There were two entry doors at the rear of the warehouse, one on either side of the two loading docks. The one on the left had a thug standing beside it, holding a silenced handgun in his right hand while smoking a cigarette with his left. His casual manner, and the fact that the man didn't look around, told him he didn't expect trouble. There was a keypad on the door next to him.

When Nedal's men and their captives approached, the thug flicked the cigarette away, opened the door, and stood aside as they entered the building—closing the door behind the person holding Milani's arm, who was the last to enter. That no one touched the keypad meant the building's alarm had been disabled.

A common misconception is that walking on sand is silent. It's not. The grains of sand rub over each other as they're stepped upon, and the air between them escapes. This emits a low but distinct noise, the level of sound determined by the speed at which the sand compacts. Hunkler was aware of this because, as a member of Italy's Afghanistan contingent, he was assigned to NATO's International Security Assistance Force (ISAF) and had been in a desert environment. Therefore, he kept his movements slow and methodical, with his noise only able to be heard within a dozen feet.

With the thug standing in the same spot and looking at the blackness stretched before him while smoking a second cigarette, Hunkler approached from the side and wrapped his arms around the man's neck, putting him in a chokehold for ten seconds. The maneuver, which he'd done many times in practice and the field, put pressure on both carotid arteries and should have rendered the victim unconscious. Instead, when Hunkler released his grip, he saw the thug had stopped breathing and was dead. He didn't know if he'd suffered a heart attack or suffocated because his body couldn't get enough air from his blackened lungs. The cause didn't matter. He was dead.

Picking up the man's silenced handgun off the ground, he checked the magazine, saw a full clip, and put the barrel under his belt. He understood that Lamberti and Acardi would throw a fit if they knew he was armed, but he wasn't going into a potential gun battle with nothing but a knife and Taser. Opening the door, he entered the warehouse.

When the four were brought into the building, they were taken to the vault, where they saw Sheik Walid Al Nahyan standing inside with the camel guide beside him. The paintings were gone.

"He's a much faster walker than I expected," Bruno said upon seeing the guide.

"He had help from the tribesmen who were camped nearby and supposed to bring your bodies out of the desert," the sheik replied in English. "I believe these belong to you," he said, opening his hand to reveal the GPS chips, which he threw on the floor before stepping out of the vault, followed by the guide.

"I see you've come off your pedestal and are speaking directly to us commoners," Bruno said, remembering the sheik only spoke to them at his residence through an intermediary.

Nedal, who believed Bruno had disrespected his boss, backhanded him across the face. The forceful impact from the bodybuilder released histamine from the damaged skin on his cheek, dilating the capillaries and turning his face red.

"Only in this situation because it's expedient. I regard the four of you as incidental people with insignificant accomplishments who should remain within your peer group."

"I didn't realize that having royal blood was an accomplishment," Bruno said. That was good for another backhand from Nedal in the same spot, further brightening the left side of his face.

"The genetic superiority of the royal family is an inherited trait. Likewise, your intellectual inferiority was preordained at birth."

"And yet, we exposed your operation."

Nedal again backhanded Bruno for a third time, with this hit cutting his lip and drawing blood. The investigator spit the blood onto the bodybuilder's sandal, garnering a look of hate that said he wanted to kill him that instant.

"You have a camera in the vault," Bruno said, deciding to stop antagonizing the sheik and putting an end to being a punching bag for Nedal.

"It was behind you. I assume the chips have GPS tracking capabilities?"

Bruno nodded that his assumption was correct.

"I'm assuming the curator came along to give you credibility and to verify an authentic from a forged painting. Who hired the three of you?"

Bruno shrugged.

Nedal was about to backhand Bruno again when the sheik held up his hand.

"You came here from Paris with the former curator of the Vatican Museums, which means you uncovered the Mona Lisa and the Vatican's art on loan to the Louvre are forgeries and that my shipping company was the method for removing them. Also, you know that the paintings formerly in this vault are authentic."

Bruno nodded that he was correct.

"How?"

"I saw on a security video that one of your transport containers was in the restoration area when experts examined the Mona Lisa. Since your shipping company transports art for the Louvre, it seemed a logical way for the forgeries to enter the museum and original works of art to leave without arousing suspicion."

"That's logical," the sheik admitted. "And that assumption led you here because you believe that I'm the culprit behind these thefts, which I am, and that I'm stealing these masterpieces for my collection, knowing that my heirs and I will be the only ones to enjoy their beauty."

"That's the prevailing theory among my colleagues, but I doubt you want these masterpieces for yourself."

"Why?"

Bruno told him.

"You're correct. While I'm behind these thefts, I don't keep the masterpieces I've stolen. The combined net worth of the six ruling families within the United Arab Emirates is over three hundred billion dollars. As you guessed, the money I could make from selling these paintings is trivial. I'm not doing it for money."

"I assume there's a massive reward for such a substantial risk. Otherwise, why would you take the chance of exposure and the expense of producing the forgeries and stealing authentic art? That must have cost millions," Bruno said.

"Tens of millions."

"Again, why take that risk?"

"You're smart enough to know that you and your associates will never leave this building alive and that your death is necessary to protect my undertaking."

"What about him?" Bruno asked, pointing to the guide.

"The same rules apply," the sheik said, nodding to Nedal, who quickly raised his silenced handgun and put a bullet in the center of the man's forehead.

"Problem solved," the sheik said, telling one of the thugs to drag the body outside. "You asked why I would take this risk," he continued.

"I'd like to know," Bruno said.

"The stolen masterpieces will go to an art aficionado who selfishly wants them for themself. In return, through a process I painstakingly established, my country will receive something that can only be purchased with political capital."

"And that is?"

The sheik was about to answer when Hunkler rounded the corner with his gun raised. Immediately, the three thugs raised their weapons and turned to face the intruder. However, before they could shoot, Hunkler sent a bullet into each, two piercing the heart and one the right coronary artery. As the colonel dispatched the thugs, Nedal raised his weapon and was about to end the confrontation when Bruno grabbed his arm and jerked it upward, sending his shot into the ceiling. Donati then joined the fray by attempting to tackle him. However, because the bodybuilder was stronger than Bruno and Donati combined, he shoved them aside with little effort. He was reaiming his weapon at Hunkler when the colonel put a round in his face, ending the confrontation. The sheik, reaching into the pocket of his kandura to remove his phone, took the next bullet from Hunkler, which pierced his heart.

"I needed him alive!" Bruno yelled in frustration.

"I thought he was going for a gun. The sheik?" Hunkler asked, never having seen him before this.

"It was," Bruno responded.

"He was wearing the same outfit as this guy, except for a different color headband," Hunkler responded defensively, pointing to Nedal.

"Did you kill all his men?" Bruno asked.

"I did."

"With no one left to question," Bruno said, giving Hunkler an irritated look, "the colonel and I will put the bodies in the vehicles and retrieve the chips. Elia, find the recordings for the surveillance cameras and destroy them. Lisette, search the warehouse for anything that might give us a clue as to where or to whom the sheik delivered the paintings. Dottore, look inside the crates in the work area and see if there's anything within them. We'll reassemble here when we're done."

"Did you find anything?" Bruno asked forty-five minutes later when he and Hunkler, who were the last to return, joined the others.

Donati went first, saying that he located the recorder for the camera feeds and, finding a hammer, obliterated its hard drive and the backup device next to it, although he didn't know what was on it.

Donais went next. "The files in the office desks are in Arabic, so I couldn't read them," she said. "But I doubt they were important, or they would have been in a more secure location than an unlocked desk drawer. Nevertheless, I took photos."

"Good thinking."

"There were five crates," Milani continued, "each with environmental units and constructed to hold two paintings. Let me tell you what else I found," he said when Donati interrupted.

"We might want to discuss that somewhere else because I think we've worn out our welcome here and don't know if someone will come looking for the sheik or if he has a nighttime patrol."

Everyone agreed.

"Let's wipe our prints off whatever we touched and get rid of this blood," Bruno said, looking at the bodies around him.

Finding cleaning supplies in a cabinet, they used bleach to get the bloodstains off the floor and a rag soaked with a commercial cleaner to remove their fingerprints.

Before leaving the warehouse, they grabbed a couple of shovels from the maintenance closet and returned to their vehicles, Hunkler volunteering to lead the way to find a stretch of desert that was far enough away from the warehouse so that the bodies would never be discovered. Because eighty percent of the country was desert, they didn't have a hard time finding an open patch of sand.

"I'm mad the warehouse didn't have a computer room where we could grab the hard drive and give it to Montanari to extract the data," Bruno said on the drive back to Abu Dhabi.

"There was no need, with only one laptop in the warehouse. If that computer was networked at all, it was to an external server the sheik controlled. It would only be allowed to input data and, seeing the DYMO printer beside it, print labels," Donati said.

"What about the paperwork required to export the art?" Bruno asked.

"Provided by the sheik or, more likely, Nedal or another trusted member of his staff."

"That makes sense," Donais said. "All that needed to be done by the warehouse employees was to affix the label and attach the paperwork handed to them."

"It was their only option, given one PC and a label printer," Donati stated.

"That level of caution is why we're at the starting line in finding out where the stolen art was going," Bruno said.

"Maybe not," Milani interjected, surprising the others by raising his voice. "I was about to tell you at the warehouse that the five crates with environmental units I saw had address labels. I have every reason to believe that they'd be inside those crates if we hadn't entered the vault and seen those paintings."

"Why weren't they put inside them and sent?" Donais asked.

"The process of immobilizing ten paintings and testing the environmental controls is time-consuming. If a painting isn't properly secured, it could be destroyed. I've seen it happen. The crates would then need to be picked up and transported, assuming they had already made those arrangements. If not, transport would need to be booked with a shipper. Those plans could be complex, depending on the destination. We were here yesterday afternoon. I'm certain the sheik found it easier to store them in another location while he took care of his problem, which was us."

"That makes sense," Bruno conceded. "Where were the paintings being sent?" he asked, cutting straight to the point.

"London."

7

It took two hours to bury the bodies deep enough so they wouldn't be found, leaving the shovels a foot below the surface of the sand and covering them by hand. Afterward, they returned to their hotels, cleaned up, and changed into their business attire—the men each wearing a suit and tie and Donais a fashionable dress. They then drove to the airport without checking out to not alert anyone that they were leaving the country. There, Donati purchased five tickets to London at the Etihad Airways counter; the flight departing in two hours at 2:20 am and scheduled to arrive at Heathrow at 6:45 am London time.

After passing through customs and immigration, they stopped at a gadget shop where Donati purchased five burner phones, handing one to Hunkler even though he had his cellphone. Bruno then called Acardi, telling him about the demise of the sheik and those with him, their burial in the desert, and their trip to London. Afterward, he and the others went to the coffee bar in the business class lounge, where each made an espresso and sat at a corner table away from the two dozen people who were spread around the room.

"It's difficult to believe the paintings went to the Emirati's London embassy," Donais said. "What was the person's name on the address label?"

"Fahad Hussain," Milani answered. "And a customs officer isn't going to open the containers because each was clearly labeled as a diplomatic pouch."

"Hussain is the distributor in the theft and shell game propagated by Al Nahyan," Bruno said. "The sheik had the perfect cover. Museum Shipping is in the business of transporting art, with the documentation attached to their shipping containers listing one or more paintings inside. Although customs inspect for drugs and other contraband, it doesn't pay attention to the authenticity of the art. They leave that to the museums. All they care about, for the most part, is smuggling and the transit of illegal items and substances."

Everyone agreed with that statement.

"Let's start the shell game," Bruno continued. "The shipping company sends the museum an environmental container with one or two forgeries. The restoration specialist, or whoever else is on the sheik's payroll, replaces the real painting with the forgery that's received, and the original work goes in the container."

"With the limitations being that the sheik can't have an accomplice in every museum, and the art has to be the right masterpiece for the forger to create a near-perfect replica of the work that's being stolen, as forgers specialize in certain types of art," Milani stated, "such as works by Renaissance masters."

"The sheik knows the extraordinary skills of the forger and only steals paintings where his expertise can be exploited," Donati said.

"And because these works won't be needed for months, if not a year or more, there's ample time to create the forgeries. When the time comes, the person on the sheik's payroll makes the switch," Milani added.

"It doesn't make a difference what museum is on the shipping label," Bruno continued, "as long as they use Museum Shipping as their transport company because every container goes to their warehouse where the original paintings are removed."

"It's their clearing house," Donais said.

"Precisely, Lisette. Let's take the Vatican's paintings. They were sent to the Louvre by a private carrier, the approximate date of their arrival announced a year in advance. The museum's restorer inspects each to document the state of the paintings when they arrive, which I've been told, is protocol. At some point, he brings them into the non-surveilled area. He then replaces them with the forgeries from the shipping container sent to the Louvre and puts an address label on it, designating its destination as the Louvre Abu Dhabi. With an active exchange program between museums, no one would believe this was unusual. The paintings are removed in the warehouse, put in the vault, and shipped to whoever," Bruno said.

"And I receive the fakes when they're returned," Milani stated.

"Why aren't they discovered at that point?" Donati asked, looking at Milani. "You have a keen eye."

"I'm embarrassed to say that I, and most curators, don't perform a detailed examination because there's a presumption that a painting returned from a reputable museum is authentic. Therefore, it's returned to the display area with the briefest of inspections, looking for damage rather than authenticity. Sometimes I'm not there when a painting is returned; my assistant will inspect and sign for it instead. If a fake is later found to be on display, the assumption is that the theft occurred at that museum and not while it was on loan," Milani volunteered.

"That makes sense," Hunkler said.

"And you said that Fahad Hussain is the distributor?" Milani asked Bruno.

"Museum Shipping sends the authentic art under diplomatic seal to Hussain. When it's received, no one but him knows there's stolen art within the containers. He delivers it," Bruno added.

"And if we know that recipient, we'll find the Mona Lisa," Donati said.

"That's the assumption. However, I doubt it will be that easy," Bruno countered.

It wasn't.

During their flight, Bruno accessed the internet and saw he'd received Montanari's message, saying he'd completed his search. He started a dialogue with the savant.

"Good evening, Indro?" he typed, knowing it was eleven o'clock in Rome.

"Where are you?"

"We're on our way to London."

"That's opportune."

"Why?"

"Because two years ago, a small fine art restoration company was established in Egham, which is outside London. Government filings list it as a sole proprietorship."

"We'll look into that. Anything else?"

"Before I go there, let me make the disclaimer that I searched for Renaissance art restoration specialists, not Renaissance art conservators."

"I don't know the difference," Bruno typed.

"I didn't either until I got into it. An art conservator works to preserve an artifact in its current condition. A restoration specialist, or restorer, returns an artifact to its original condition."

"A subtle but clear distinction," Bruno noted.

"I focused on the latter and didn't include conservators because it would have significantly expanded the search and didn't seem to fit your intent."

"Good thinking. What did you learn?"

"It's a fluid career choice, with restoration specialists frequently changing employers and professions."

"Why?"

"The average fine art restorer earns around forty thousand dollars a year. In major cities, the salary escalates to almost seventy thousand dollars which, considering the increased expense, brings their net down to what the average restorer earns. Subsequently, it takes only a small boost in wages or a change in benefits to get them to move. Many leave this profession as they get older or have families to find a higher-paying job. Therefore, although they might appear unemployed because they no longer work in this field, they have another profession. The turnovers and change of professions immensely complicated my search."

"I get it, Indro, and I appreciate how you busted your ass to get me what I wanted, knowing I gave you a bag of lemons and you handed me a glass of lemonade," Bruno said, understanding that Montanari had the information he needed but wanted him to know that it didn't come easily. "How did you narrow it down to the person in Egham?"

"Seven restorers fit my search parameters. One left a major museum and retired in Prague; another retired in Geneva. One married an American and moved to New York, while another teaches in Tokyo. The last person who left a major museum and didn't go to another works for a small restoration company in Singapore."

"And the seventh was the person in Egham. Send me whatever you found on them. I owe you."

"I'll put it on Donati's tab," the savant typed.

Bruno was about to share the information he'd received with the others, but they were asleep. Deciding to wait until they landed, he sent emails to Acardi and Lamberti, telling them what he learned from Montanari and that, after they checked into their hotel, they'd visit the restorer living in Egham. Bruno then closed his eyes and didn't open them until he felt the less-than-gentle landing of the aircraft at Heathrow, the flight arriving fifteen minutes early.

Before their journey, Donati booked two suites at the Wellesley Knightsbridge Hotel, two hundred yards from the UAE's embassy. As traffic was moderately heavy, their taxi arrived at eight-thirty. Once they checked into the hotel and received their room keys, Hunkler and Milani in a two-bedroom, and the investigators in one with three, they walked a block to Harrod's to buy personal items. When they returned and cleaned up, Hunkler and Milani went to the larger suite, where room service had delivered coffee, juice, and breakfast pastries. As the others were indulging, Bruno relayed his conversation with Montanari. When he finished, Donati was the first to speak.

"If the paintings went to London, it's reasonable to assume Hussain delivered them within or near the city," he stated. "That this restoration specialist lives nearby is too coincidental to be happenstance and worth investigating."

"How will we get Fahad Hussain to tell us where he sent the masterpieces? And why should he? He has diplomatic immunity and can give us the finger instead of helping us incriminate him and the late Al Nahyan," Hunkler said. "He may also warn whoever has the Mona Lisa that we're here looking for the masterpiece, causing them to go far enough off the grid so that we'll never find the painting."

"Which is why we're going to Egham first," Bruno stated. "If we're correct about the restorer, they'll know the identity of the person receiving the stolen art and the location of the Mona Lisa. If we come up empty, we can discuss how best to approach Hussain."

"How far from London is Egham?" Hunkler asked.

"Let me look," Donais said, finding out the town of seven thousand was a twenty-two mile, forty-two-minute drive on the M4 motorway.

"Do we rent a car?" Donati asked.

"Does anyone feel comfortable driving on the opposite side of the road?" Bruno asked.

When Sheik Walid Al Nahyan, Nedal, and those accompanying him didn't return to the residence by 7:00 am, the head of his residential security tried tracking the phones of the security guards who accompanied him because neither the sheik nor Nedal had that program installed on their devices. He came up empty. He next looked for the signals from the GPS tracking devices installed on the vehicles, seeing they were at the warehouse. Unwilling to wait the two hours until the shipping company's employees arrived, he ordered three guards to accompany him there.

Finding the front door unlocked with the alarm disarmed, and with weapons drawn, they searched the warehouse but found no one inside. Unable to contact the sheik and his security detail, and with their vehicles abandoned and the warehouse unsecured, he feared something terrible had happened to his boss. Knowing he didn't have the resources to conduct a wide-ranging search, he called the police.

At 9:00 am, with law enforcement discretely searching for Al Nahyan and getting nowhere, the petite woman, who learned of the situation from the residence guards, called the head of security and told him that she suspected the four were behind the disappearance and possible deaths of the sheik and his security team.

"You're telling me that an old man, a woman, and two middle-aged men who look better-suited to eating a pizza than neutralizing my security team, and without firearms, were responsible for possibly killing my men and the sheik?"

"That's what I'm saying."

"What leads you to this preposterous assumption?"

"His Highness tried to kill them in the desert, but they escaped and evaded capture—skills acquired by those with military or tactical experience," the woman replied.

"I was told about the failed attempt, which is why the sheik went to the warehouse. He believed they'd return because they'd seen some of the missing paintings in the vault." The line went momentarily quiet while the security chief pondered what was said and what to do next. Breaking the silence, he thanked the woman for her comments, which surprised her because thank you was a phrase she didn't believe existed in his lexicon, and ended the call.

With no leads and law enforcement seemingly unable to get traction on their search, the security chief ran with the petite woman's assumption, upping the ante by telling the police captain he'd previously spoken with that the foreigners murdered Sheik Walid Al Nahyan and his security detail. Even though he didn't know what happened to his boss, he wanted to make their crime as heinous as possible. He added they should be considered armed and extremely dangerous, advising that the captain's men should protect themselves by shooting them on sight. The security chief knew those instructions would ensure that whatever the four uncovered would die with them.

A short time later, the captain called back and told him that because they had clothing and personal items in their suite, he believed the fugitives, as he now called them, were still in Abu Dhabi and probably sightseeing.

"These people are not tourists; they're killers," the security chief angrily responded. "Send a countrywide notice that they're wanted for murder and are to be killed on sight."

The police captain, who had just been asked to kill the foreigners on sight without there being a body, did as he was told. Because the security chief's employer was the leader of Abu Dhabi's royal family, he could always pin whatever happened on the rent-a-cop, knowing the royal family would give him cover for killing the foreigners. He subsequently issued the arrest warrants with the notation that the fugitives could be shot on sight if an officer felt threatened, knowing that comment meant they were unlikely to be taken alive. The captain went one step further to cover his ass if they escaped the country. He requested the nation's National Central Bureau, or NCB, to send critical crime information notices to Interpol's General Secretariat. These would be published on Interpol's website, with the NCB assigning a specific color to the requests for cooperation from police in member countries and asking them to share crime-related information or take appropriate action.

There are eight levels of Interpol notices, each delineated by a different color. A red notice is the highest, seeking the whereabouts or arrest by local authorities of the person in question with a view to extradition. However, because the fugitives were accused of murdering a member of the royal family and his security detail, the notices included the same warning the captain placed on the arrest warrant, giving officers the option of killing rather than arresting the four if they felt their lives were threatened.

Acardi didn't need a call from Pia Lamberti to let him know that Bruno and his colleagues were in serious trouble; both told of the red notices at approximately the same time. Acardi, calling Hunkler's phone, told Bruno.

"They have an hour or two before the British discover they've cleared immigration and trace them to their hotel, which will have already entered their passport information into their computer system and forwarded it to the government's database," Lamberti stated. "When they receive it, the police will arrest and hold them, if they're not killed on sight, while the extradition request from the Emirati goes through the courts."

"If they don't find the sheik's body, they can't prove he's dead," Acardi said.

"That doesn't mean they can't hold them until they find something else to charge them with while searching for the sheik and unraveling what they're doing in Abu Dhabi. That's if they're captured alive and survive in jail. If they do, the only way to resolve the situation with the Emirati is to prove the sheik's involvement in the theft of art," Lamberti said. "Linking him to stealing the Mona Lisa, the Vatican's paintings, and other masterpieces will get them to drop their investigation because that revelation would make the royal family radioactive in the UAE's dealings with the nations whose paintings were stolen."

"Asking why Museum Shipping was sending containers filled with art to their London embassy could start the dominoes falling," Acardi added.

"Except only one person alive knows there was art inside them—Fahad Hussain. He'll deny it, and without proof, further accusations by us will be discredited."

"Bruno's going to Egham to speak with a restoration specialist who moved there after quitting the del Prado in Madrid," Acardi said.

"I wish I could interrogate him."

Acardi, who'd seen her interrogations, knew she'd eventually get the truth, although he may not survive the encounter.

After Bruno concluded his call, he informed the others about the red notice. "That means we can't leave the country by public transport, check into a hotel, or use our credit cards without being arrested or shot by local authorities. For now, Colonel Hunkler is the only person unaffected."

"But we're checked into this hotel," Milani responded. "The police will know we're here."

"Not yet. Acardi found out about the red notice at eight o'clock our time, thirty minutes after we arrived at the hotel. The notice will take time to filter down to the local police," Bruno, who retired as a chief inspector with Venice's Polizia di Stato, responded. "I don't know the British system, but if it's the same as Italy's, a nationwide notification to local law enforcement takes two or more hours."

"Also, Interpol can't arrest anyone," Donati, a former chief inspector with the Polizia di Stato in Milan, added. "It relies on local law enforcement to act on its requests."

"You're saying that we have approximately two hours before the police know we're at this hotel," Milani said, looking at Bruno.

"Probably longer. Although the hotel copied our passports, that data isn't entered into a centralized database, so the police have no automated way of knowing where we're staying. Instead, upon receiving an Interpol notice, the local authorities, London's Metropolitan Police Service, send a BOLO to hotels in their jurisdiction asking to be contacted if the persons listed in the notices are guests or attempt to check in. It's not unusual for it to take as long as four hours from when local authorities email the BOLO until someone at the hotel reads it and checks their guest database. I'd estimate the earliest local law enforcement would know we're at this hotel would be at eleven this morning, and it could be this afternoon if the hotel staff is busy and doesn't check the emails."

"Because the hotel arranged for our car service, they'll know where we've gone and notify authorities once they receive the notice," Donais said.

"The same is true for a rental car. A taxi seems our only option," Donati said.

"Can we all fit in one vehicle?" Hunkler asked.

"London cabs can carry five people, three on the back seats and two on the fold-downs facing opposite directions. There's plenty of room for our bags in front of us," Donati answered, familiar with the city's cabs from frequent trips to London with his parents.

After Bruno called the concierge and canceled their car and driver, the five left the hotel without bothering to check out. They walked a block up the street to an ATM where Donati got as much cash as possible from several of his credit cards. He then hailed a cab, giving their destination as Egham.

Forty-five minutes after leaving the center of London, their taxi pulled in front of the business address that the savant emailed Bruno—a pack and ship company in a small strip of commercial businesses.

"I don't know how suite one thirty-three could be inside a pack and ship," Hunkler said, looking at their destination. "Montanari must be wrong."

"He's never wrong," Donati countered before Bruno could respond.

"Can you wait for us?" Bruno asked the driver, unsure if they could get another taxi to return to London because none were within view.

Once the driver said he'd keep the meter running, the five walked into the small establishment, which was devoid of customers. As they entered, they saw the number one thirty-three above one of the mailboxes to their right.

Bruno approached the middle-aged person behind the counter and asked if he could speak with the owner. The man pointed to himself and said he was the owner, janitor, and handyman. He next asked if he had a way to contact the person renting mailbox number one thirty-three because they only had this address and not a phone number."

"The foreigner?"

"Is he a foreigner?" Bruno asked.

"He has a Spanish accent."

"What do you know about him?" Hunkler inquired, flashing his Vatican badge, which impressed the owner, who didn't look at it closely.

"Interpol?" the owner asked because of their accents. When Hunkler didn't answer, the man assumed they were agents and began talking.

"He uses this as his company's business address, but he works out of his home and someplace in Virginia Water, which is in northern Surrey," the man volunteered. "That's an area for the extremely wealthy."

"Do you know him?" Hunkler continued.

"Everybody in a town this size knows everyone. He's gone all day from Monday through Wednesday."

"Today is Wednesday. How do you know?"

"Because a car picks him up. The only road into or out of town is the one out front. I always see him puffing on a cigarette because the rear window is down."

"Who sends the car?" Hunkler asked.

The man said he didn't know.

"But you know his address and phone number," Bruno said.

The man wrote them down on a piece of notepaper and handed it to him.

Bruno, believing they'd gotten all they could, thanked the owner and left.

The red notice filtered down to London's Metropolitan Police Service at 10:30 am, the police sending an email blast to every hotel an hour later. Because it arrived at checkout time, and the staff of the Wellesley were busy with guests departing before the noon deadline, no one read the MPS notification until one. Upon seeing it, the general manager checked the hotel guest list, found the four, and phoned the police. Thirty minutes later, a CO19 team, the equivalent of SWAT in the United States, entered both suites using the keycard provided by the front desk, finding them empty.

Because the hotel was in Knightsbridge and close to Harrods, one of the most famous department stores in the world, and a tourist mecca, the armed CO19 force entering the hotel attracted a crowd and was recorded on multiple phones. Local news organizations received dozens of these recordings minutes later, afterward bombarding the MPS with requests for information on the raid. Although the police were silent on the matter, a front desk clerk at the hotel gave a local reporter a copy of Interpol's red notices. Moments later, the faces of the four were on social media.

When Hunkler's cellphone rang, he saw "no caller ID" appear on his screen. Because Acardi and Lamberti both prevented the display of their phone number to whoever they were phoning, he accepted the call, expecting it would be one of them. He wasn't disappointed.

"Let me speak with Bruno," Acardi said, the sound of his voice indicating he was under stress.

The colonel handed Bruno his phone.

"Have you looked at social media in the last fifteen minutes?" he asked.

"I haven't," Bruno replied.

"The red notices and photos of you, Donati, Donais, and Milani have gone viral."

"That makes it more challenging because Britain has an extensive facial recognition system that people consider Orwellian. I don't think they implemented it in small towns, but you never know."

"Tell me you're close to finding the Mona Lisa because the walls are beginning to close in on your team."

"Discovering its location is a process. We're going to speak with a restorer, who we suspect is employed by the person who has the painting."

"When?"

"As soon as I get off this call. If we find the Mona Lisa and the Vatican's paintings, any thoughts on how we'll get them out of the country? It may be a hot extract," Bruno said, meaning the bad guys could be chasing and shooting at them.

"Lamberti has that covered. Let me know when you learn anything. And Mauro, get to the bottom of this quickly and don't get caught. If any of you are, you'll probably be killed before you can be extradited to the UAE. If you're lucky and survive, the outlook for a long life doesn't improve. Since you're being accused of the death of Sheik Walid Al Nahyan, the patriarch of Abu

Dhabi's royal family, if the three-judge panel convicts you, they can vote to put you in prison for life or send you to a firing squad. You can bet the royal family will have their thumb planted firmly on the side of the scale that's less favorable to your longevity."

8

The forger's name was Pasqual Ortega. He wasn't especially fond of living outside London, finding the weather cold and damp in the winter, the food bland, and the women blander, in stark contrast to his native city of Madrid. He moved to Egham for the boatload of money he received from his client and purchased a house as close as he could to the nosebleed-priced real estate of Virginia Water, where his benefactor lived. At twenty-eight hundred square feet, the one-story residence was nearly three times the size of the average British home. Because it sat fifty yards from the road and was surrounded on the other three sides by a row of tall trees, it provided him with the privacy he required.

Although the house was relatively new, he extensively renovated its interior to meet his artistic needs. He began by ripping out the wall between the two bedrooms at the rear of the residence and installing dark wooden flooring. Afterward, he replaced the three exterior walls of the newly created room with floor-to-ceiling glass and the roof over it with a giant skylight. The purpose of these extensive renovations was to ensure that the area in which he painted was illuminated by northern light, which provided a consistent brightness without shadows because it didn't change direction during the day.

It was seven in the evening when Ortega got out of the white Mercedes S580 and walked down the charcoal-colored brick pavers that led to his front door. The forger was twenty-eight years old, five feet six inches tall, slim, and had medium-length black hair. He wore black Lululemon pants, a matching long-sleeved shirt, and black OC athletic shoes. The house was dark as he unlocked the two deadbolts and opened the heavy wooden door. After entering, he switched on the lights by habit and, without looking around, walked into the living room. The five people staring at him from the couch and surrounding chairs caused him to jump back in fear and stumble to the floor.

"Who are you?" he demanded, picking himself off the ground with his hands trembling.

"Private investigators. We want to ask you some questions about a missing painting," Bruno said, that comment drawing a look of concern from Ortega.

"You want to question me in my house?"

"Yeah."

"Get out."

"Not yet."

Ortega looked at the five facing him, didn't like the odds, and decided to answer in a way that skirted what he did. "I'm an artist," he replied after a brief pause.

"You're being modest," Milani said. "The two paintings on easels in the room at the end of the hall are excellent forgeries that would fool most of those who purport to be art experts."

The forger took his eyes off the group and focused on the curmudgeon. "They're replicas. They're forgeries if I paint them with the intent of selling those paintings as the originals. What's illegal is breaking into my home. Did I leave the door open, or did you pick my locks?"

Hunkler said it was the latter and admitted he was the culprit.

"As you said, selling replicas is acceptable if you represent them as such. However, it's considered forgery if one substitutes a replica for authentic art. It's also theft," Bruno continued.

"I'm not responsible for what the person buying my painting does with it."

"Cute, but ultimately an unconvincing argument to a jury. What are the odds that the few paintings you forged are the only ones switched out of the five thousand paintings in each museum in which substitutions occurred?" Bruno asked.

"You have no proof of my involvement."

"Proof is an often misunderstood word. Circumstantial evidence is considered proof from which someone could infer the facts in question," the former chief inspector said.

"What circumstantial evidence?"

"I'll let Dottore Milani explain. He was the curator of the Vatican Museums for five decades."

Ortega's mouth went agape in surprise.

"The disassembled furniture that I saw in the garage is from the Renaissance period, exactly what you'd need to create the stretchers used in your paintings." The curmudgeon began, explaining to those accompanying him on their search of the garage that stretchers provided the wooden framework to which an artist attached the canvas.

"The tools next to the furniture are also from the Renaissance period and were known to be used during that time to cut and shape stretchers. In the corner of the garage are jars in which iron nails are oxidizing in salt water. They'll eventually deteriorate enough to use in attaching the canvas to the stretcher."

"I strive for authenticity," the forger interjected.

Milani didn't respond, continuing his analysis in a calm voice.

"In your bedroom, I found canvases scraped with pure acetone, taken from the plastic bottle beside them. I assume these came from lesser-known Renaissance-period artists, and you're reusing their canvases to defeat carbon dating techniques. I also saw you're making pigments, which I assume will be chemically era-appropriate, even going so far as to grind lapis lazuli to produce a blue dye. I also want to compliment you on the forged Leonardo on one of those easels. You're extremely good at duplicating his techniques, although they're not perfect."

"It's impossible to replicate his genius."

"This is what I mean by circumstantial evidence," Bruno said.

"Call it what you will, although all it proves is that I'm obsessed with selling replicas as close as possible to the original."

"You said you were investigating me because you think I'm involved with the disappearance of a painting."

"That's why we're here," Bruno responded.

"Which painting?"

"The Mona Lisa."

"What?" the forger said in astonishment. The speed at which he said it betrayed his genuine surprise. "It's been stolen and replaced with a forgery?"

"With your forgery," Donati declared.

"Very few forgers have the talent to replicate the Mona Lisa at a level capable of deceiving museum curators. That you are intimately familiar with the painting techniques of Leonardo, as exemplified by the Bacchus, makes you the focus of their investigation," he said, pointing to the others in the room.

"I know you have no reason to trust me, but believe me when I say I've never painted a replica of the Mona Lisa."

Feeling the conversation wasn't going anywhere, Bruno decided on another approach. "Do the names Sheik Walid Al Nahyan and Fahad Hussain sound familiar?" he asked.

The question remained unanswered because the look on Ortega's face was all the verification he needed.

"We know the sheik's Museum Shipping company was the conduit to swap your forgeries for the original works, and that Fahad Hussain at the UAE embassy in London received the stolen paintings and arranged for them to be delivered to the person who ultimately possesses these masterpieces. Honestly, do you believe these people of stature will take the fall and leave someone like you untouched? We both know that's never going to happen. Like it or not, you'll be linked to these thefts. If the police don't find that association on their own, they'll help. When we leave here, we're going to visit Hussain and see what he has to say. I'm betting he'll give you up in a heartbeat."

"Don't see him."

"Why?"

The forger began fidgeting, and sweat accumulated on his forehead—telltale signs of duress that didn't go unnoticed by the three investigators and Hunkler.

"He'll kill me. He's an elitist leach who treats me as if I'm gum under his shoe, once telling me he'd do anything to protect himself and the sheik, implying that I'm a dead man if I consider betraying them."

"The irony is that he's a diplomat and can murder you without consequence," Donais said.

"I know."

"Tell us everything, and we'll keep your name out of our report. However, there are three conditions," Bruno said.

"I'm listening."

"You give us a list of the forgeries you painted and who commissioned them. Second, help in our investigation, and don't hold anything back. Third, retire from, using your words, painting replicas."

Ortega agreed.

"Let's start at the beginning," Bruno said. "How did you get into this business?"

For the next two hours, Ortega explained he was a talented but starving artist in Madrid with dreams of painting masterpieces comparable to the legends of the Renaissance. He lived in a tiny apartment above a butcher shop, where he was paid to clean blood and animal remnants off the floor and sanitize the equipment every night. During the day, after getting a few hours of sleep, he'd go to museums to study the Renaissance masters before returning to his apartment to try to duplicate their techniques, colors, and hues, as well as the pigments and paints used during that period. After ten years of hard work, he found he could visually replicate the masters to perfection.

Spending nearly every penny he had, he purchased the supplies necessary to duplicate several of his favorite masterpieces and brought them to local galleries, hoping they'd be displayed so that tourists or wealthy businesspeople would buy them. Out of the thirty galleries he visited, only one agreed.

His first sale took a month, with the unlikely buyer being the Earl of Warenne. The renowned owner of Renaissance masterpieces, who had a habit of looking through local galleries when traveling, saw Ortega's replica of one of his paintings. Amazed that someone could so accurately duplicate it, he purchased it and the two other replicas on the condition that the gallery owner would arrange a meeting with the artist. The following day, the earl met Ortega, flew him to London, and chauffeured him to his seventeen-hundred-and-fifty-acre estate in Virginia Water, an hour outside the city.

"The earl is known to have one of the finest private collections of Renaissance art in Europe," Milani said. "How could you replicate one of his works without physically seeing it?"

"His masterpieces are famous and have been photographed numerous times with high-resolution cameras. Also, those Renaissance artists have painted other works, some of which are in the Museo del Prado in Madrid. Studying those imbued me with the knowledge to replicate the earl's painting, which was always one of my favorites."

"Why would he want to buy a replica if he owns the original?" Donais asked.

"I didn't ask and didn't care. I needed the money and was being paid extremely well for doing what I loved."

"Why do you paint in two places, here and at the earl's estate? That seems odd," Donati commented.

"I painted at his estate until I finished duplicating the last of his masterpieces, after which I expected to be unemployed. Therefore, I was surprised when he told me I'd now be replicating famous paintings hanging in various museums using my knowledge of the artist and digital images viewed on my computer. He also increased my pay. For someone who'd been poor all their life, I didn't question the offer. I took the money."

"Are the paintings in the back room for him?" Donais asked.

Ortega confirmed they were.

"And is he the only person who's commissioned your paintings?"

"The only one."

"Are his masterpieces displayed throughout the residence?" Donati segued.

The forger responded by saying that the earl's art was displayed in the single-story wing of the mansion perpendicular to the main house.

"We'd like to see it," Bruno said.

"I'd like to go out with Ana de Armas, but neither is likely to happen," Ortega responded, drawing smiles from the five.

"Are outsiders permitted inside the mansion?"

"If they're fixing something. The residence was built in seventeen seventy and, from what I could see, requires constant maintenance. There's rarely a time I've arrived at the estate or left when one or more maintenance crews weren't there. That said, I spend my day in the art wing, which has restricted access."

"How restrictive?" Bruno asked.

"It requires a key to enter."

"A key? Not a digital passcode typed into a keypad or biometric sensor?"

"A key," he repeated.

"He must have security guards," Bruno said.

"Four. Two patrol outside the mansion and two monitor camera feeds in the security office, to the left of the foyer."

"What prevents thieves from overpowering them, stealing the paintings, and escaping before police arrive? That doesn't seem difficult," Hunkler said.

"The four Rottweilers who make the art wing their home and will kill anyone who enters without the earl."

"What happens when the earl travels?"

"The dogs are kenneled, and additional guards are brought in to stand in front of the door and the impact-resistant windows at the back of the art wing, the only way to get into the area."

"That works," Hunkler admitted. "The dogs don't bother you?"

"They don't bother anyone as long as the earl escorts them into the room. Only a few outsiders are allowed in the art wing. Mostly, they're bankers."

"Bankers?" Donais questioned.

"They periodically inventory the masterpieces."

"How do you know they're bankers?"

"They wear three-piece suits and have a stick-up-their-ass attitude. Beyond that, I heard them speaking about loans and collateral but didn't pick up the entire conversation."

"Did they see you painting?"

"No. I have a studio at the end of the art wing, which is a duplicate of the one at home. The earl introduces me as his restoration specialist, which seems to go over well with the bankers. While they're in the wing, I spend my time looking closely at the masterpieces and go back to painting when they leave."

"I need to make a call," Bruno said, going into Ortega's art studio and using his burner phone to call Acardi. After updating him on what they'd learned, he asked for a data search, receiving a return call three and a half hours later from the chairman of Italy's domestic intelligence agency.

"Let me give you the background on the Earl of Warenne's family so you can understand how the bankers got involved with his estate," Acardi started. The earl's commoner name is Edward Stanley. He came from a wealthy family who made their fortune in the late eighteenth century by farming their estate's land and investing heavily in overseas businesses that offered lower wages and emerging markets. They were astute at spotting trends and used their profits to purchase Renaissance masterpieces, which they believed would significantly appreciate over the years. Not trusting banks because the laws governing them at that time were very different from today; they kept their remaining capital in gold, precious jewels, and cash. That investment philosophy proved correct and spared them from the stock market crash of eighteen twenty-five and the failure of twelve banks."

"Smart ancestors. How rich were they by today's standards?"

"Billionaires in today's money, and millionaires during their time. The family thrived until the late nineteenth century when, two years after purchasing a controlling stake in the biggest steel factory in Germany, the government nationalized it just before World War One. The factory was destroyed during the war."

"That hurt."

"The family was still financially sound, even after Wall Street's crash in nineteen twenty-nine and the British drought of nineteen thirty-five. However, maintaining the estate and their lifestyle consumed cash. Their investment hardships continued after World War Two with the destruction of their assets in France and Spain. Eventually, they were forced to pledge their masterpieces and estate as collateral to obtain successive bank loans, the lender being King's Heritage Bank."

"The earl inherited an indebted estate and the proverbial money pit without the financial resources to sustain the estate or pay down the debt," Bruno summarized.

"That's it. But here's where it gets good. In nineteen seventy-seven, the earl's mother moved her loan from King's Heritage

Bank to the International Merchant's Bank of Abu Dhabi's newly established branch in London, which solicited their business and offered a favorable interest rate."

"Why?"

"Only the earl can tell you. But the Emiratis are shrewd businesspeople. They wouldn't take the risk unless they were receiving something of greater value than the interest from the loan or the assets they'd receive on default."

"And you know what that is."

"I think so. The only thing the earl had going for him was that his family had generationally been on the board of two national museums, meaning they'd interact with those of extensive wealth."

"I'm betting that Sheik Walid Al Nahyan was on the bank's board," Bruno said.

"Yes—linking the earl to him."

"How large is Edward Stanley's bank loan?" Bruno asked.

"Seventy-eight million dollars, with the principal due in a balloon payment three years from now. Several years ago, a puff piece by a London magazine estimated the value of the earl's art collection as more than one hundred and fifty million dollars. If you couple that with the estate, the earl is over-collateralized."

"But short on cash," Bruno said. "What are his annual interest payments?"

"Five million dollars a year," Acardi replied. "Add that to an estimated one hundred thousand dollars a month to maintain an estate of this size, and you can understand the significant amount of cash needed every month."

"I can't see how Edward Stanley can be our collector because, by definition, that person must be a deep-pocketed. The earl is trying to keep his head above water. My guess is that if Milani looked at his masterpieces, most would be forgeries and that he sold the originals under the table to get badly needed cash," Bruno said.

"And the bankers, who probably aren't the world's best at detecting forgeries, see the correct number of masterpieces in the art wing and assume they're authentic."

"That's what I believe," Bruno said.

"The sheik's involvement is in getting the forgeries from Stanley and shipping them to the museum with the original works. He then arranges to send the stolen art to Hussain, who gets it to the earl. He sells it to our collector. The sheik must know he's screwing the bank by taking away their collateral," Acardi added.

"He's a billionaire, or was before Hunkler killed him. His involvement wasn't about money; it was about something else," Bruno said. "Edward Stanley is the only person who can fill in those blanks and lead us to the Mona Lisa. We need to speak with him."

"How?" Acardi asked.

"Considering the large loan amount, the International Merchant's Bank of Abu Dhabi would have the clout to send bankers on a moment's notice to audit their collateral. He won't be able to contact the sheik for obvious reasons, who could have called it off."

"And you're the banker?"

"I was thinking of Donati and me," Bruno replied.

"Milani will also need to go because you both couldn't recognize a masterpiece from a paint-by-numbers painting without him. However, your Italian accents may be a problem since Edward Stanley will be expecting someone from the London branch of the bank or an Emirati."

"It can't be helped. With the red notice, time is against us. Even a casual glance from someone on the police force could end our investigation and put us behind bars."

"Do you look like bankers?" Acardi asked.

"Astoundingly, yes."

"I'll brief Lamberti and ask her to get you a meeting with the earl tomorrow."

"How will she do that?" Bruno asked. "It's past midnight in Rome."

"I don't know, but she was appointed the country's intelligence czar because she routinely does what most of us consider impossible."

"And frequently asks the same of us," Bruno said before ending the call, wondering how they would find and return the Mona Lisa to the Vatican in less than two weeks while staying off the grid and avoiding being arrested or killed by police.

9

It was well known by anyone who knew Pia Lamberti that she only slept when it didn't interfere with work. Subsequently, she was at her desk reading NATO intelligence reports when Acardi called at 12:20 am and listened in silence as he repeated his conversation with Bruno.

"Whoever has the Mona Lisa, and presumably the other stolen masterpieces, will be difficult to find. I doubt those involved in the thefts know anything more than their compartmentalized role," she said once he'd finished.

"Edward Stanley must know who's buying his paintings and the stolen works. He's the middleman," Acardi said.

"That's an assumption we can't afford to make without additional information, which I expect Bruno to provide."

"In that respect, do we have a relationship with the Emirati bank to get Bruno, Donati, and Milani a meeting with Stanley?" Acardi asked, segueing to the reason for his call.

"I don't need one. When I phone the Emirati Minister of Finance, I'm not requesting that he set up this meeting; I'm demanding it. The UAE enjoys its wealth and is considered the Switzerland of the Middle East because they're non-threatening to other countries. Consider what would happen if the sheik's role in the theft and forgery of world masterpieces became known.

The global trust that took decades to establish would evaporate instantly."

"We have no physical evidence the sheik was involved in these thefts. We only have allegations of wrongdoing."

"I'm not getting into specifics. A mention of the sheik's company having a contract with the museums where the thefts occurred, and the shipping containers ending up at the London embassy should be enough. One look at the number of diplomatic pouches sent to London will establish the credibility of our accusations."

"When will you phone the minister?" Acardi asked.

"Following our call."

Acardi looked at his watch. "It's 3:30 am in the UAE."

"That's not my problem."

World leaders, important individuals within governments, corporate CEOs, and other centers of influence share their phone numbers and contact information with similar hierarchies to facilitate expeditious contact. Whoever is charged with making contact on behalf of one of these individuals has access to their cellphone number, the number of their aide or other in-between, or a government or corporate communications center charged with verifying the identity of the person on the phone to determine if the call is legitimate and should be forwarded. As prank contacts are commonplace, the usual practice is for the receiving party to phone back the purported caller on a number they know is legitimate.

Because Lamberti had never spoken to the Emeriti Minister of Finance, and her position within the Italian government was not on any organizational chart, she phoned President Orsini's aide and asked that she contact the minister and transfer the call to her. It was unnecessary to give the aide, who was familiar with Lamberti's position and President Orsini's trust in her, the reason for the early-morning conversation. Subsequently, the aide phoned the minister's assistant, woke him up, and requested an urgent conversation with his boss.

"Can it wait until midday?" the semi-awake assistant asked.

"If it could, I wouldn't be up, nor would I be calling you at this hour," the aide rebuked. "It's urgent. Can the minister speak English, or will an interpreter be needed?"

"He attended Cambridge and speaks six languages. His English is substantially better than yours," was the frigid response before the line went dead.

When the minister phoned back, the president's aide transferred the call to Lamberti, who introduced herself and explained that she worked for the president and directed a government intelligence function. She didn't elaborate.

The minister, believing he would be speaking to President Orsini on a time-sensitive matter of mutual importance, was highly vexed at the bait and switch and let Lamberti know he didn't appreciate the deception.

"Deception is why I'm calling," she countered. "I've learned that Sheik Walid Al Nahyan, a member of the royal family, has been stealing Renaissance masterpieces from major museums and replacing them with forgeries, deceiving the institutions exhibiting these works and the governments who ultimately own them."

"That's preposterous."

"Just as preposterous as using his shipping company in Abu Dhabi as the conduit for the switch and sending the stolen paintings to Fahad Hussian in your London embassy?"

"Both accusations are without substance."

"And yet, easily verifiable by you to prevent an international scandal that involves an Emirati bank."

"Explain," the minister said, fully awake.

"Ask yourself why the sheik would send shipments of art in diplomatic pouches to an official in your British embassy and what that official did with them."

"Diplomatic pouches from Sheik Al Nahyan to a foreign embassy wouldn't be unusual."

"Not even if they all come from Museum Shipping, the sheik's art delivery company, go to the same embassy official, and the transport is made within days of a theft?" Lamberti replied, not knowing if her accusations were entirely true, but suspecting they were.

"And the involvement of an Emirati bank?"

"The International Merchant's Bank of Abu Dhabi's London branch facilitated a loan to Edward Stanley, the middleman receiving the stolen art from your embassy official."

"I'm sure many Britons receive loans from this bank. Some might call that accusation grasping at straws. You've made serious accusations against the head of one of our royal families. Do you have proof, or are these merely the assumptions of an intelligence director?"

"I have photos of stolen paintings at the sheik's warehouse and the diplomatic labeling on the shipping containers showing them going from Museum Shipping to your embassy in Britain. I also have a confession from the person who forged these paintings implicating Sheik Walid Al Nahyan and your embassy official, Fahad Hussain," Lamberti said, not mentioning that Ortega's confession was verbal to ensure there was no paper trail documenting the actions taken by Bruno and his team.

"Perhaps I can have someone ask the shipping company's employees for their perspective. They're more forthcoming when speaking with another Emirati than a foreigner."

Lamberti didn't believe those conversations would involve the government cordially asking questions.

The minister was silent, and Lamberti heard him take several deep breaths.

"Let's assume what you've said is true. Why is the Italian government involved?"

"Because two stolen masterpieces are from the Vatican Museums, and one is on loan to it from a major European museum," Lamberti answered.

"Since you appear to have known about these thefts for some time, why the urgency of this call? What aren't you telling me?"

The intelligence czar momentarily thought before answering, deciding she'd never get the minister to aggressively move forward unless he knew the end game. "I haven't told you that the major European museum is the Louvre and that the stolen painting that was replaced by a forgery is the Mona Lisa. I don't want to create a diplomatic furor. My only goal is the recovery of the masterpieces."

"What do you propose?"

Lamberti replied that she needed to have the manager of the London branch of the International Merchant's Bank of Abu Dhabi call Edward Stanley and say that later this morning, three persons representing the bank would inspect their collateral for insurance purposes.

"How does that help you find your paintings?"

"It allows my team to enter Stanley's residence, confront him, and find the person to whom he forwards the stolen art. They should have the Mona Lisa and the Vatican's paintings, or know who does."

"Don't mention my nation, members of the royal family, or government officials."

"Because the thefts weren't publicly disclosed, neither will their recovery. There will be no documentation of our actions."

"What are the names of the three people?"

Lamberti provided them and said the earl should expect their arrival at ten. "I'll also need your NCB to rescind, along with two other names, crime information notices to Interpol's General Secretariat," she said, giving him those names.

"Why did we issue the notices to Interpol?"

"The local police made wrong assumptions. How that occurred is too lengthy to discuss at this hour. If I'm going to keep your country out of this fray, I need the five red notices rescinded. If my team is apprehended, we both stand in the light."

The minister agreed, afterward saying that he had several conditions.

"As I would expect."

"Even though I take you at your word as to the lack of documentation accompanying your efforts, if it's necessary to blame one or more people for these alleged crimes, they can't be Emirati."

"No Emirati will be implicated."

"Then our business is concluded. Keep me apprised of the situation, only much later in the morning," the minister said, ending the call.

Lamberti leaned back in her chair, contemplating her next move. "Bring the car around," she told Zunino several minutes later. "But first, I need to get something from the kitchen," she said, leading the way to her forty-eight-inch Sub-Zero refrigerator.

It was two in the morning when Indro Montanari, who was up late finishing a computer program for a client, was startled by the doorbell. Dressed in his daily uniform of Levi jeans, a long-sleeved black uncollared shirt, and athletic shoes, he started toward the front door, intending to look at his intruder through the peephole.

"Indro, I see your lights are on. Open up," Lamberti said before the computer-savant got to the door.

Montanari had an innate fear of the nation's intelligence czar who, from past interactions, had a habit of arriving at his home unannounced to have him perform a series of hacks and other illegal activities to support covert operations. Although she said she'd provide cover to protect these activities from being discovered or investigated and hide his identity, he believed that if someone needed to take the fall, he'd be the last one standing when the music stopped.

As he opened the door, Lamberti entered the house, followed by Zunino, who handed the computer-savant a box of cannoli and a carton of Red Bull. Montanari didn't ask how she got the tasty Italian pastry at this hour, knowing that the intelligence czar liked the Sicilian desert and kept an ample supply at her residence.

"Bruno and his associates have a problem," Lamberti said without preamble.

"Mauro always has a problem," he responded before opening the box and taking a bite of his cannoli.

"Irrespective, we need to figure out how to help him find the person who has the stolen art, which would include the Mona Lisa," she said before bringing him current on what was happening in Britain.

As the savant listened, he grabbed another pastry and quickly devoured it, followed by a Red Bull.

"Any ideas?" Lamberti asked once she finished.

"Bruno had the best idea when he had me search for restoration specialists. Whoever is acquiring these masterpieces isn't going to let them deteriorate. They'll have an appreciation for these works and maintain them in pristine condition. Given what we know, money isn't an issue, and I assume they've collected art for some time and have employed one or more specialists during that period."

"Do you have the search you did for Bruno?"

"It only produced one name of consequence."

"Pasqual Ortega?"

"For your purposes, he's a dead end. He works for Edward Stanley and not this collector. However, all searches depend on the data pool."

"Meaning?"

"The information retrieved depends upon the parameters that are set. With Bruno, the timeline searched was two years."

"And that wasn't long enough, or we would have had more than one name," Lamberti stated.

"Probably. "Precisely. Since the person behind these thefts isn't likely a recent art aficionado, we need to go back decades."

"How long will that take?"

"To modify the algorithm and conduct the search? Several hours."

"I'll wait."

The algorithm's timeline was three decades. It completed that search in three hours, the program categorizing the results into four groups. The first was restorers who left museums or public institutions for higher paying jobs, their names taken from employee rosters, and their pay scales from historical hiring posts at or near the time of their employment. The second group listed those who retired or died. The third gave restorers who changed careers. Group four were restoration specialists that were off the grid, meaning they seemingly vanished. That group had one name—Ulrick Schmidt. Montanari did a deep dive on him, handing Lamberti a printout of the information he'd retrieved.

"Born in West Berlin in nineteen sixty; attended the prestigious Berlin University of the Arts, which was founded in sixteen ninety-six, graduating number one in his class; worked for the Gemäldegalerie museum in Berlin, which has one of the world's leading collections of European paintings from the thirteenth to eighteenth centuries; employed there between nineteen eighty-one and nineteen ninety-five after being certified as a Renaissance restoration specialist," Lamberti read aloud. "He later became that museum's chief restoration specialist for Renaissance art. His fame gained traction after articles were written on him in numerous publications, all praising his ability to restore masterpieces without altering the creator's look."

"Impressive," Montanari admitted.

"At thirty-five years of age and the height of his career, he goes off the grid," Lamberti continued. "There's no record of a passport, driver's license renewal, death certificate, marriage license, name change, or anything else that will give us a clue what happened to him."

"My algorithm searched every centralized database in the EU that contained public records. If you want to delve into restricted government records, I'll need to hack them individually."

"What about public transport databases, such as airlines and trains? They might give his travel history and a clue to his whereabouts," Lamberti suggested.

"That's a good idea. But I'm not sure how long they store those records. Let me look," the savant said and began typing on his keyboard.

Lamberti walked to his desk and stood beside him.

"Airlines and maritime operators maintain travel records for five years and train operators for one," he read from the data on his screen. "After that time, they transfer this information to EU government databases, where it's stored for an additional fifteen years. Given that he left the Gemäldegalerie museum twenty-eight years ago, his travel records no longer exist in any database."

"What about family?" she asked.

The savant did another search. "He's an only child, as were his parents, both of whom were born in Berlin. His mother's maiden name was Becker. The couple married in Berlin when he was twenty-one and she was twenty. In 2004, Ulrick's father died in Berlin of emphysema at age sixty-five. There's nothing further on his mother, Karin," he said, summarizing what he'd found.

"Let's stop here," Lamberti said, seeing from a clock on the savant's wall it was 6:15 am. "We'll reconvene at noon after Bruno meets with Edward Stanley. In the meantime, see what you can find on Karin Schmidt."

Once Lamberti and Zunino left, the savant grabbed another can of Red Bull and began searching for Karin Schmidt, whose public information ended with the death of her husband, something he didn't believe was accidental. Whatever happened after becoming a widow, she wanted it to be kept secret. That meant finding anything on her would be extremely difficult, an assumption that proved entirely correct.

10

Bruno, Donati, and Milani took a taxi to the earl's estate, arriving at precisely ten. The mansion was a three-story rectangular structure, fifteen thousand square feet to the floor, built with Portland stone—a white-grey limestone quarried on the Isle of Portland in Dorset, England. Perpendicular to it was the ten thousand square feet art wing, sheathed in stone that was less grey than the main part of the house because the limestone came from a later cutting.

A butler escorted the three to the earl's office—a medium-sized room painted in a subtle cream shade, with a white ceiling bordered by an opulent cornice. At the rear of the office was an antique desk, in front of which was a cream-colored sofa decorated with red fringe cushions and a red-cushioned wooden chair on either side.

The Earl of Warenne didn't stand when they entered and wordlessly pointed to the couch. Once seated, the butler, whose posture was as rigid as if he was in military formation, stood beside the door and stared straight ahead.

"Can you explain why I was awoken at an unconscionable hour and told to make my loan collateral available for inspection by you three? Out of respect, the time and date should have been coordinated to suit my schedule."

"My apologies," Milani replied, feeling better suited to work with elitists because he'd seen more than his share during his tenure at the Vatican Museums. "The bank has a new insurance carrier, and they've given us only the briefest time to re-certify the assets of our major clients."

"Are you all Italian?" Stanley asked with a look of puzzlement upon hearing his accent.

Milani confirmed they were.

"Why are you here instead of my local banker?"

Thinking fast, the curmudgeon responded the bank had a new policy that required the recertification of loan assets by consultants not associated with the financial institution or client.

"You're consultants?"

"For the art division of an Italian insurance carrier," Milani acknowledged.

"That makes sense," the earl agreed.

"I suppose you want to see everything—the inside of my home, the stables, greenhouses, and so forth."

"Only the art," he countered. "The land and structures are self-evident."

The earl seemed happy with that response. "Would you like to see their provenance and valuation?"

"After we view the paintings."

"This shouldn't take long. Follow me," the earl said, leading them to the art wing and, after removing an ornate brass key from his pocket, opening the door. Inside, four growling Rottweilers charged toward them.

"No," Stanley commanded, bringing each of the one hundred thirty-pound dogs to a halt ten feet in front of them.

"Do they live in this wing?" Bruno asked, the adrenalin rush subsiding.

"For the most part. They have a large, windowed area with floor beds at the back, where they stay unless they're playing. It's not unusual to see their toys scattered about the galleries. They're exercised several times a day and stay outside until they get restless and want to return. They like being in this wing and protecting it because it's their home. As you can see, it's brightly lit, a timer dimming the overhead lighting at nighttime."

The ten thousand square feet room they entered was divided into three galleries, each representing, as Milani would later tell them, a period of the Renaissance. On its walls were paintings by Leonardo da Vinci, Michelangelo, Raphael, Donatello, Sandro Botticelli, Hieronymus Bosch, Giotto di Bondone, Albrecht Dürer, and Jan van Eyck.

Milani broke off from the group and began looking at the paintings as the earl led Bruno and Donati through the wing, explaining the background of some of the works. The curmudgeon caught up with them twenty minutes later.

"You have a spectacular collection."

"Thank you," the earl replied.

"I've never seen better forgeries," Milani added, his voice indicating the certainty of his findings.

Edward Stanley gave him a hardened stare, which softened once he realized the octogenarian was the real deal and that no amount of bluster, intimidation, or denial could make him change his mind.

"What makes you believe that?" he asked, curious how he came to this conclusion when other so-called experts had examined the same forgeries and came away believing they were viewing the authentic masterpieces.

The curmudgeon explained that the technical aspects of the paintings he viewed were inconsistent with the techniques employed by the artists, and that what he saw would be imperceptible to someone not intimately familiar with their methodology.

"Give me examples," the earl said.

Milani explained the minute inconsistencies in the paintings he viewed compared to the original works. The detailed analysis surprised Edward Stanley.

"What did you do before becoming a consultant?" the earl asked.

"I was the curator of the Vatican Museums for fifty years before I retired."

"That explains your expertise. Others who came to validate my works viewed them from a distance, having already accepted they were original works of art because they saw their provenance and certification of authenticity by renowned experts before entering this room. However, even if I had shown those to you, I'm sure you would have looked just as carefully at these works and come to the same conclusion—that every one of my paintings is a fake."

"The quality of these representations is so good they would have fooled most of my former colleagues," the curmudgeon responded.

"What about you two?" the earl asked, looking at Bruno and Donati. "What did you do before becoming consultants?"

"We're not consultants. We were police officers before becoming private investigators," Bruno answered.

"Is that so?" he asked, his eyebrows raising in surprise. "And you're investigating me?"

"We're investigating the theft of the Mona Lisa," Bruno answered.

"The Mona Lisa has been stolen?"

"And other famous works."

"What does that have to do with me? I didn't steal it."

"Why not? You're involved in the theft of other masterpieces."

The earl looked nauseated. "Let's continue this discussion in my office," he said, leading them out of the art wing.

"Are you going to report what you saw to the bank?" the earl began once everyone was reseated, and he dismissed the butler from the room.

"That's up to you," Bruno replied.

"You'll need to explain that statement."

"It depends on what we learn from you about the theft of the Mona Lisa."

"I told you. I didn't steal it."

"But you know who did."

"I know who could, but not who did," the earl countered.

"Let's start with how you got involved with Fahad Hussain and Sheik Walid Al Nahyan."

"And in return for these self-incriminatory explanations?"

"Let's not play games. You're already incriminated by the forgeries in the art wing."

Edward Stanley acknowledged that was true.

"If you help us, neither the banks nor law enforcement will be told what we learn. We're only after the Mona Lisa. You're ancillary to that, but only if you cooperate."

"And if I don't?"

"Don't go there. That path benefits neither of us."

"Quite right."

"Let me first understand the landscape. Tell us why we saw forgeries rather than the collection of masterpieces you and your family are renowned for."

"That begins with understanding my family history," Edward Stanley replied. "My family was one of the wealthiest in Britain until two world wars destroyed their overseas investments, the crash of Wall Street in nineteen twenty-nine evaporated their stock portfolios, and a countrywide drought devasted their crops. These events consumed cash reserves and cut my family's cash flow far below what they needed to maintain the estate and keep up appearances. Inevitably, my ancestors had to swallow their pride and obtain a loan from a local bank, which my mother later moved to the International Merchant's Bank of Abu Dhabi when they offered a very favorable interest rate."

"Why would they do that? Rate reductions are only made when a bank receives something of value, such as conducting other business with the client," Donati said. "Therefore, as a single-purpose borrower, you must have had something significant to offer."

"That's very perceptive, and you're correct. This middle-eastern bank, which came to the land where snobbery and arrogance were invented and still prevails, needed an anointment of respectability to establish a foothold in Britain."

"Your family's endorsement," Bruno said.

"Yes. They advertised us as borrowers, giving them credibility and acceptance. Hence, the favorable interest rate. By this time, our financial problems were an open secret. You can't hide the calamities that beset us—the slowness of payments to the trades, the layoffs of staff, and the lack of estate maintenance. Even though we had massive assets, our cash flow was insufficient to cover overhead. The annual cost of maintaining this estate is one and a half million dollars. That doesn't include expenses such as equipment replacement or unforecasted maintenance. However, even though the banks didn't require the repayment of principal until the end of the loan, the interest payments combined with the annual costs to sustain the estate proved formidable. When my ancestor's optimism on the expected cash flow from outside investments didn't materialize and debts mounted, our family had two choices—sell assets or borrow. We chose the latter."

"You inherited quite a problem," Bruno said.

"That problem was an eighty million dollar debt when my mother passed away—not the legacy I anticipated. Confronted with this, I knew that selling the masterpieces was the only reasonable way to obtain the cash to pay down the debt and cover my overhead. I was in preliminary discussions with Christie's to auction them when I went to Madrid to escape the pressure and happened upon a young artist's magnificent reproduction of one of my paintings. Although I don't have your expertise," he said, looking at Milani, "I could see his brilliance. I viewed my family's masterpieces daily and couldn't discern a difference between this artist's reproduction and the original work. That's when I came up with the idea of selling the originals piecemeal and replacing them with his forgeries. If I couldn't tell the difference, I didn't believe the cursory inspections by the so-called art experts sent by the bank could discern it either. I went on the dark web, eventually finding a buyer, intending that some proceeds from the sale of an original masterpiece would cover overhead, with a majority set aside to pay down the estate's debt."

"Why not sell them all at auction and be done with the debt and interest payments?"

"British arrogance. British vanity. A desire to remain in my snobbish peer group. Call it what you want. However, the results would be the same: the debt would have been satisfied, and the masterpieces sold."

"You still had substantial overhead, even without the interest payments," Donati pointed out.

"The estate is largely composed of agricultural property. That revenue makes it self-sustaining and provides a modest revenue cushion."

"But you discovered that once you sold your first masterpiece, the buyer substantially lowered the price for your next sale," Milani said.

"How did you know?"

"It's a common tactic in the illicit sale of art on the black market."

"My naiveté was obvious to the buyer. Given the new pricing, I wouldn't earn enough from selling my masterpieces to retire the loan. The only remaining option was to sell the estate."

"There wasn't another black market buyer who'd pay more?" Donati asked.

"The buyer told me that if I didn't exclusively sell to him, he'd anonymously expose the sale to my lender."

"That put you at the mercy of his pricing," Bruno said. "Enter the sheik who, knowing your financial situation because of the successive loans your family required over the years, offered a solution. Did he know about your black market sales?"

"He knew about them from chatter on the dark web. He didn't know the name of my buyer."

"Knowing that you violated the terms of his bank's loan, he took advantage of the situation. What did he want?" Bruno asked.

The earl nodded, indicating that the assumption was correct. "Antiquities," he answered.

"Your family's?"

"The UAE's," the earl clarified.

"I'm confused," Bruno responded, Donati and Milani also echoing their lack of understanding. "He didn't care that you were replacing the bank's collateral with forgeries?"

"Not in the slightest. I'm a trustee of the National Gallery and Chairman of the National Museum Directors' Council. These positions were accorded to my family generations ago due to our societal position, collection of masterpieces, and generous donations to the arts before we became poor. Because of my status, the sheik wanted me to spearhead the return of antiquities taken from the UAE and brought to Britain."

"Since these antiquities couldn't be purchased, they needed to be voluntarily returned," Bruno stated, understanding why the loan was less important to the sheik than the return of his country's heritage. "Why wouldn't the British government give them back with an apology?"

"If we did that for every antiquity we'd spirited out of foreign countries during our colonialization period, the British Museum would be empty. We only do it by exception when my government wants something in return or public pressure forces the repatriation."

"Explain that in more detail," Donati said.

"The British Museum has been the world's largest receiver of stolen goods. Many of its more than eight million artifacts, including the Benin Bronzes, Rosetta Stone, and the Parthenon Marbles have been taken from other countries. Some of these artifacts are from the UAE, and the Emiratis have been trying to get them back for some time. Because of my position as Chairman of the National Museum Directors' Council, the sheik felt he could leverage me to pressure my colleagues to return these antiquities."

"Did you?" Bruno asked.

"I discovered that the museum officials didn't care about the UAE's antiquities. They were forgotten and only came to their attention when seen in a computerized inventory of items in storage. My suggestion, which the rest of the council accepted, was to give them back to the Emiratis with an inordinate amount of fanfare as a sign that our countries could work out their historical differences. This would create goodwill at home and abroad and defer pressure to return other nations' antiquities. Of course, the British are second only to the Chinese in having circular discussions without resolution, and we have no intention of returning anything else, much less huge attractions such as the Rosetta Stone or Parthenon Marbles."

"The sheik gets his nation's antiquities in exchange for ignoring the sale of the bank's collateral?" Donati asked.

"Better. In exchange for forgiveness of the loan and re-establishing my family's wealth."

"Therefore, you don't need to sell masterpieces anymore," Bruno said.

"I'm afraid that ship has sailed. I sold all my paintings."

"Now that I know what the sheik was after, I don't understand why he would steal works of art from museums. Correspondingly, why would you do this if you were going to be out of debt and the cash flow from your agricultural lands, and the money set aside from the sale of your paintings, could support the estate? Why take the risk of discovery?" Bruno asked.

"While the sale of crops would keep the estate alive and provide me with a reasonable lifestyle, and the money I received from selling my paintings was significant, it wasn't enough to return my family to prominence. Because of my financial difficulties, there have been discussions about removing me as a trustee and council member, replaced by a billionaire and substantial donor to the arts who didn't have my financial baggage. Even though I have a royal title, I was increasingly looked upon as a commoner living off their ancestry. While that's not uncommon in England, it was frowned upon because of the positions I held. A substantial donation to the arts, coupled with annual donations, would put to rest allegations of my financial demise."

"I think I understand," Bruno said. "The sheik was involved in the thefts because of the other condition you gave him."

"Exactly, and he put together the mechanics of how that would occur."

"Using Museum Shipping to smuggle forged art into the museum and the authentic works out," Donati said.

"The timing couldn't be better. The Louvre licensed its name to the museum in Abu Dhabi and was receiving numerous works of art to fill its exhibition spaces. That's when the sheik started Museum Shipping to take advantage of the movement of art. I had the forger. He had a way to move the stolen art and the money to bribe museum employees to steal targeted works."

"He's a billionaire. Why didn't he wire you money to an offshore account?" Milani asked.

"He would have preferred that, but as he explained, he had an office full of accountants and attorneys overseeing his business dealings. He couldn't wire large sums without selling some of his assets, which I assume would be stocks or bonds. Their liquidation, with a corresponding wire to an unknown offshore account, would raise too many questions among the professionals he employs, making it hard to keep the transaction from being questioned. In contrast, the theft and shipment of the art involved a handful of people. If his company was somehow implicated, he could deny knowing anything about it."

"And the sheik delivered the stolen art to you through the Emirati embassy in London, and you sold the art," Bruno said.

"That was the mechanism."

"Who's the buyer?"

"The same black market entity who bought my paintings, only I negotiated better terms of sale. Afterward, he gave us a list of artists and paintings he wanted, which was our focus."

"Does your black market buyer have the Mona Lisa?" Bruno asked.

"If they do, it didn't come from me."

"Given the thefts, I sense the sheik didn't stop at building you a nest egg," Bruno said.

"He saw how easily money could be made from these thefts. Besides the thefts for which I received the funds, the sheik also sent other stolen works to the same black market buyer."

"You didn't have a problem with that?"

"We were both making money, and he was doing the heavy lifting."

"Did you speak to the buyer, or was everything handled on the dark web?" Bruno asked.

"Once the buyer was notified that we acquired a masterpiece on their list, their attorney handled the receipt of the stolen art and wired the money upon verification of authenticity."

"What constituted verification?"

"Authenticity tests before transferring the art and wiring of money. There could hardly be paperwork establishing provenance since the paintings were stolen."

"We need the attorney's contact information."

"I have his phone number."

Bruno saw the country code was 44, meaning Great Britain, and that the area code was 01865, which the earl explained was Oxford and its surrounding area—fifty miles from the estate.

"I don't think it will do you much good," he commented. "It's an answering service."

"It's a start," Bruno stated. "How did you deliver the art?"

"The attorney sent a truck."

"And they did the authentication at that time?"

"Yes. Inside the truck was a miniature lab with a spectroscope, X-ray machine, and infrared reflectography equipment. The authenticator was in the car that followed the truck."

"After your art passes visual and electronic inspections, then what?" Donati asked.

"The person who authenticated the art makes a phone call and says the painting is authentic. Afterward, he tells me to check my offshore banking account to verify the receipt of funds. When I say the money is there, the truck driver and his two helpers put the painting into an environmentally controlled container, secure it, and leave."

"Did you notice the country of origin for the license plates on the truck or car? Donati asked.

"There was no license plate on either vehicle."

"They probably removed them before they came up your drive," Donati volunteered. "Were their accents British?"

"The person who authenticated the painting was the only one who spoke. He had a German accent."

"What about the attorney?"

"Their accent was French."

"How long did it take from when you called the attorney until the truck arrived at your estate?"

"On average, two weeks."

"That means they didn't necessarily come from Britain," Donati said. "What now?" he asked, looking at Bruno.

"That's a good question."

When Bruno called Acardi and gave him the attorney's phone number, they agreed it would be too risky to contact the answering service and ask questions about their client, fearing they'd report the call to them.

"Can Montanari hack the answering service's system to get the information? He should be able to penetrate their server faster than a hot knife through butter," Bruno asked.

Acardi agreed that was the easiest way to get what they needed and called the savant. Twenty minutes later, he phoned Bruno.

"The good news is that he found that the answering service is in Dorchester on Thames, a village nine miles south of Oxford. The bad is that it doesn't have a website, so there's nothing to hack. The only evidence of their existence is a small advertisement in the British Telecommunications yellow pages for Oxford."

"The attorney could have chosen this answering service because it doesn't have an internet presence, making it impossible to hack and discover their client's contact information," Bruno theorized. "Is there anything written about them on the internet?"

"Not even a client review. That's why Montanari decided to call, pretending to be a chiropractor relocating from London to Oxford."

"How did that go?"

"He found it's a family business owned by two sisters who run it from home. Their four daughters work there, and their clients are primarily healthcare professionals. When Montanari told them he was worried someone could hack their system and get his personal information, saying this so that he could find out if they had another internet site, he was told with a laugh that they keep their client list and phone numbers on a Rolodex."

"No one uses a Rolodex anymore," Bruno replied.

"They do. It gets better. They don't maintain a record of calls, explaining that they write the message on paper and read it to their client."

"They don't send a text?"

"The sister who spoke with Montanari said they wanted to ensure the client got the message. A text may or may not be read."

"That makes sense."

"Afterward, they throw the message away," Acardi continued.

"But the Rolodex would have the attorney's contact information," Bruno stated.

"If we knew their name."

"You might not need that. If it takes two weeks for the truck to arrive at the estate, it must be coming from some distance. We look through the Rolodex to find anyone using the service who's not local. There can't be many."

"How do you plan to get access to the Rolodex for any length of time when the business is in their house?"

"I don't know," Bruno admitted.

"Neither do I, but we need to try because the attorney is our link to the person we suspect has the Mona Lisa. Use Lisette," Acardi suggested. "She's personable and exudes trust when she speaks with people, qualities you and Donati lack."

"Thank you," Bruno sarcastically replied.

"You're welcome. Finesse isn't a core strength for either of you. Hunkler can watch Ortega while Lisette speaks with the sisters. And Mauro, don't you or Donati give her advice on how to handle this. She'll do fine without it."

"Because we're not personable nor exude trust?"

"Precisely."

Lisette Donais phoned the answering service. After saying her husband had called earlier and she'd like to speak with them before engaging their services, she was told they'd welcome her visit, and a time was set for 1:30 pm.

Donais' taxi took ninety minutes to get from Egham to Dorchester on Thames, pulling in front of the single-story red brick house ten minutes early. She asked the driver to keep the meter running and wait. The nineteen fifties home was two thousand square feet, had a semi-circular gravel driveway, and was extensively landscaped with flowering plants. Donais rang the doorbell and was greeted by one of the sisters, who led her to the office, which was the first room to the left as one entered. The twelve-by-twelve-foot space had a long table against the back wall, on which ten, twenty-four-button multi-line phones sat, each button with a three-digit code atop it. In the center of the table was a Rolodex and a legal pad.

"This is it," the sister said. "My sister, me, or one of our daughters is in this room 24/7. When one of the lines ring, we take the message, go to the Rolodex, find the client, and call them."

"It seems you have quite a few clients," Donais said, looking at the bank of phones.

"We've been at this for decades and have a loyal clientele, with half our business coming from the university's medical and health sciences departments. The other fifty percent are doctors, dentists, chiropractors, physical therapists, and other area professionals."

"What's the cost for your services?"

"One hundred dollars a month. There's also a one-time fee of one hundred fifty dollars to British Telecommunications for running a phone line to our home and a monthly fee of twenty-five dollars for that line."

"That seems reasonable," Donais said. "I don't see a computer. I'm curious. How do you run a business without one?"

"This isn't London. We're a local company serving a small area. We started before PCs were widely adopted, and, given how smoothly everything runs, we couldn't see a benefit or reason to migrate to them. Our system doesn't need software updates; it can't get a virus or crash and works when we lose power. We have laptops and cellphones, but we don't see a need to introduce technology into our business. Simplicity is best."

"If it isn't broken, don't fix it,' Donais said.

"That's what we believe."

"I see the phone numbers are written on a piece of paper to the right side of the buttons, and beside each are the same three digits that appear on top. Is that a client number?"

"No. It corresponds to the client's Rolodex card, which gives us their contact information and the number on which they wish to be called with their messages. The phone number you see on the paper is the incoming call number, given to patients and so forth by the professional."

Donais, who'd memorized the attorney's number, found it as she was speed-reading the pieces of paper. One hundred ten was printed on the button next to it. "Would it be possible to get a glass of water?" Donais asked, coughing for effect.

The sister said she'd be right back and left the office.

When she left, Donais removed the phone from her purse, went to Rolodex card number one hundred and ten, and photographed both sides. The phone was back in her bag by the time the sister returned.

After thanking the woman and saying she'd speak with her husband, Donais returned to the taxi and texted the photos to Bruno and Acardi. The attorney's name was Philippe Pastor, and he had a London address. It took the savant two hours to glean the internet of whatever he could find on him, after which he called Acardi, who conferenced Lamberti into the conversation.

"What have you got?" Lamberti asked.

"Nothing, because Pastor's Paris phone number came from Hushed."

"What's Hushed?" Acardi asked.

"It lets the user, who could be anywhere in the world, get a fictitious local phone number, make private calls, and send anonymous texts while hiding their identity. As a precaution, I did a comprehensive search for anyone named Philippe Pastor who lives in Paris or the surrounding areas. Dozens have that name, but none is an attorney."

"The sheik is dead, the earl doesn't know the name or location of the buyer, and we know nothing about the buyer's attorney who's involved with every purchase. Where does Bruno go from here?" Acardi asked, disappointment evident in his voice.

"To the south of France," Lamberti replied.

"Why?"

"Because that's where he'll find Karin Schmidt and, with any luck, her son Ulrick."

"Did I miss something?" he asked, surprised Lamberti hadn't told him about this until now.

"Indro called while you were speaking with Mauro. He found that in 2004 Karin Schmidt moved from Berlin to Saint-Paul-de-Vence, France, following the death of her husband. We have her address."

"I've never been there," Acardi said.

"It's a medieval village twelve miles from Nice and a former gathering point for artists like Matisse, Picasso, and Marc Chagall; philosophers like Jean-Paul Sartre; and the Hollywood elite. Even the most basic home would cost well over one and a half million dollars. I considered purchasing a summer villa in the area," she said, surprising Acardi. "How does a museum restorer get that much money?"

"Family wealth?" Acardi volunteered.

"The family hasn't historically displayed wealth. Karin Schmidt and her husband lived in a four hundred thousand dollar Berlin home, which she sold last year," the savant stated. "She could be the beneficiary of her husband's life insurance policy or retirement fund."

"I believe she moved to be with her son. He would have known about this small commune because he had been involved with art his entire life. He may even have fantasized about living there. They might be sharing this house, or he may live nearby. Since Ulrick Schmidt is the only Renaissance restoration specialist who seems to be off the grid, he's our prime suspect for working with the person who has the Mona Lisa," Lamberti said. "Tell Bruno to get to Heathrow. I'll make the reservations."

Acardi called Bruno and told him they were wasting their time chasing the attorney, but that his suggestion of finding the restoration specialist associated with the buyer of the stolen art might have paid off.

"Karin Schmidt, formerly Karin Becker, lives in Saint-Paul-de-Vence, France. We believe her son Ulrick is the restorer we're looking for and is living with his mother or close to her."

"If Schmidt isn't retired, we can follow him to his employer," Bruno said.

"That's what we thought. Have you ever been to Saint-Paul-de-Vence?"

Bruno said he hadn't.

"I'm looking at it on my computer. It's a town of meandering alleyways and centuries-old stone cottages on a hill overlooking the Mediterranean. However, its compactness will make it difficult to surveil Karin Schmidt's residence 24/7 without being conspicuous."

"Unless we're staying in town," Bruno said.

"That's what Lamberti thought. She booked you into the La Colombe d'Or Hotel, less than two hundred yards from the Schmidt residence. You're ticketed on the six o'clock British Airways flight from London to Nice tomorrow morning, getting you there a little past nine. Nice is in the same time zone as Rome. A minivan from Sixt has been reserved for you, and the hotel is six miles away."

"What about Ortega?" he asked.

"Make him understand that this is a two-way street. If he keeps silent on everything that's happened and stops painting forgeries, we'll refrain from telling the authorities in Britain, France, and Italy about his activities."

"According to Milani, he's extremely talented. Maybe we can find him employment or put him in a training program to be a restoration specialist," Bruno offered.

"That puts his talents to good use. I'll speak with Lamberti."

"What about the red notices? Have they been rescinded?" Bruno asked.

"The rescissions have reached the local level in Britain."

"And France?"

"They've yet to confirm at the local level."

"Meaning we'll find out when an immigration officer sees our passports and either waves us through or puts us in cuffs."

"That sums it up nicely," Acardi said before ending the call.

The distance from Egham to Heathrow is nine miles which, driving in traffic, takes thirty-three minutes. At four in the morning, it took half that time. The five picked up their tickets at the check-in kiosk and went through customs and immigration without incident. Finding that the shops and restaurants were open because the busiest airport in Europe was a 24/7 operation, they went into a tech shop and purchased five iPhone 14s, making the day of the half-asleep salesperson behind the counter. Although they couldn't get their cellphone numbers and carriers transferred to the new devices, the salesperson set them up with EE, a partnership of two telecommunications giants that most Brits considered the best carrier in the UK.

They boarded their flight at five-fifteen, the plane landing at the Côte d'Azur Airport five minutes early. After deplaning, and with their aircraft at the furthest gate, they walked down a long corridor that ended at two immigration lines. It was 9:15 am.

Bruno was the first to approach the border surveillance officer, who placed his passport on the automated reader. Expecting a green light, the officer did a double take when he saw it flashing red. He pressed a button under his counter, and seconds later, two armed police officers arrived. They cuffed Bruno without explanation and took him away. The same scenario played out for Donati, Donais, and Milani, with Hunkler being the only one to make it through immigration. He called Acardi.

There was no presumption of innocence for the four; the police having received red notices indicating they were extremely dangerous. Each was taken to a holding cell and brought separately into an interrogation room over the next two hours. After determining that English was the common language between them and their interrogator, they were asked a litany of questions, the police not buying the cover story that they were on vacation.

Captain Edgard Bence sat in on the failed interrogations. He was thirty-two years of age, bald, stood five feet eleven inches tall, and was thick-chested without being fat. The unmarried officer had a chisel-cut face that was clean-shaven, a muscular physique from years of working out, and a deep voice that some would associate with years of smoking, although he'd never touched a cigarette.

Following the last interrogation, Bence returned to his desk to notify the National Central Bureau that four red-notice fugitives had been apprehended and that he would start the paperwork for their deportation to the UAE. However, as he brought up the Interpol website to enter this, he saw their names were no longer in the system. That's when he leafed through the half-inch stack of faxes and other papers that had accumulated in his inbox, finding the recission of the notices. Seconds later, he received a call from the director general of the national police, who'd been asked by Acardi why three Italian citizens with valid passports and no custom or immigration violations were in custody. With no alternative but to admit that he didn't look at the red notice recissions, Bence was verbally eviscerated.

"I have to tell the Italians that my department screwed up and apologize. This display of incompetency to another government is embarrassing and tarnishes the image of the French police," the director general angrily retorted. "If the Italians press the matter and choose to make this an international incident, it will end my career because I'll be the sacrificial lamb offered by our government to them."

"I understand," Bence replied.

"Do you? If that happens, you'll be behind me in the unemployment line. Release the four and start kissing their asses," the director general said before ending the call.

Ten minutes later, Bruno and the rest of the team were given back their items and escorted by Bence, who spoke passage English, to the Sixt car rental counter. During that five-minute walk, the captain apologized profusely and said if they needed any favor during their stay, all they had to do was ask. He handed Bruno his card with his cell number. "The call from your government to my superior didn't help my career. If you file a complaint, it's over," Bence said.

"We're former law enforcement officers," Bruno replied. "We understand mistakes happen, and we have no intention of filing a complaint against a fellow officer. Let's forget about this and call it a day."

"I appreciate that," Bence said, apologizing again and pointing to the card he gave Bruno. "If you need anything."

Hunkler, in the rental car seating area, had watched what was happening with a grin. "You've had an interesting morning," he said, taking bottles of water from a plastic bag and handing them out.

"Thanks for calling Acardi," Bruno said, knowing that triggered the chain of events that led to their release.

"The clerk told me our rental car is in the parking lot on the other side of that door," Hunkler said, dangling the keys and pointing to it.

As they followed him, Donati saw the octogenarian was walking slowly and appeared weary from the combination of the early morning flight and the excitement of being arrested and interrogated. He grabbed Milani's carry-on bag off his shoulder and placed it over his. Bruno slowed his pace and gently held onto the upper part of the curmudgeon's left arm, acting as a crutch to make it easier for him to walk.

"He doesn't look good," Donais told Hunkler, the pair five yards ahead of Milani and slowing down to match his speed.

"We're almost there."

When they got to their vehicle, Hunkler sat in the driver's seat and entered the hotel address into the navigation system while Bruno helped Milani into the front passenger seat of the seven-seat VW Touran so that he could have more legroom. Afterward, the others took whatever seat was open.

The drive to the Colombe d'Or Hotel, perched atop a hill overlooking the Bay of Cannes, took sixteen minutes. The rustic-looking stucco-walled hotel was elegantly landscaped with flowering plants and lush vegetation, some of which clung to walls, turning them into a carpeted layer of green leaves. The Golden Dove, the English translation of the hotel's name, began as a neighborhood café and bar with an open-air terrace that offered a spectacular view of the water. As its popularity increased, it added hotel accommodations, gradually expanding to its current capacity of thirteen rooms and twelve suites.

The check-in process was efficient, and before going to their rooms, the five agreed to meet on the terrace in thirty minutes for lunch at one. Because Bruno was restless, he used that time to do a solo reconnaissance of Karin Schmidt's home, the address having been texted to him by Acardi.

Although the town first came into existence between the tenth and eleventh centuries, making it one of the oldest on the French Riviera, the buildings on both sides of the cobblestone street on which Bruno was walking were built during the sixteenth century. Schmidt's two-story villa was halfway down the street. The steep-roofed, two-story French provincial residence had a beige stucco exterior, two large arched windows with white shutters, and a heavy wooden front door stained chestnut brown.

Bruno casually walked past it and proceeded down the hill—circling back to the hotel using the street below the residence and arriving at five minutes to one. Entering the terrace restaurant, he selected a corner table that gave him a view of Schmidt's residence, the other diners preferring to look at the Mediterranean Sea instead. Once the rest of the team was seated, one server handed out menus while another poured chilled Acqua Panna Natural Spring Water into each person's glass.

Because they hadn't eaten since the night before, they quickly ordered, everyone choosing the special of the day—a fish entre on a bed of risotto—a northern Italian rice dish cooked until it reached a creamy consistency. Once the server left, Bruno pointed out Schmidt's home and told them what he saw.

"Since none of these residences have garages, everyone parks their vehicle on the street. That means we should get a good look at them," Bruno said.

"If Ulrick lives there with his mother," Hunkler pointed out.

"If not, let's hope he visits her frequently."

"How do we plan to surveil the residence without drawing attention?" Milani asked, having regained some of his vigor.

"We'll do it from here," Bruno answered. "The four of us will work in shifts, taking a cellphone photo of whoever enters or exits the house. The telephoto lens and high megapixel function on our new phones should give us a closeup."

"How long are the shifts?" Hunkler asked.

"Every three hours, daybreak to sunset," Bruno responded. "Outside of that time, I'll assume that they're either asleep or in for the night."

"What do we do once we get their photos?" Milani asked.

"We text them to Acardi to find out if they're in any of our databases and if that produces something about them that we don't know. While he's doing that, we follow them. If it's Ulrick Schmidt, we hope he'll lead us to the person with the Mona Lisa. If it's his mother, we're looking for a rendezvous with her son. Either way, we need to find a nearby parking space for our minivan so that we can get to it quickly. Therefore, the keys need to be with whoever is watching the residence."

"I'll slip a few euros to the valet to keep it parked on the hotel's drive," Hunkler said.

Their discussion continued until the food arrived, after which they devoured their food while keeping a cautious eye on the residence.

12

Karin Schmidt left her home at two that afternoon as everyone was having an espresso. Donais was the first to see her and took photos of the eighty-three-year-old pulling a mini four-wheel shopping cart out the front door. The octogenarian, who walked with a slight stoop, wore a flower-patterned long-sleeve dress, whose fashion had come and gone several decades earlier, and comfortable shoes that one might see on a waitperson. She was five feet six inches tall, thin, but not overly so, and had her gray hair in a bun.

"I'm on it," Donais said, getting up from the table to follow her. Fifteen minutes later, she called Bruno, saying that Karin Schmidt had gone to a small market at the end of the street.

"If you can do it without attracting attention, get a closeup of her face," Bruno said.

Twenty minutes later, the woman returned home, Donais trailing at a prudent distance. She'd just entered the house when a white Peugeot 208, the company's newest generation compact car, parked just ahead of her, the driver getting out of his vehicle and entering the residence. Donais snapped photos of the man and the car's license plate.

"Ulrick Schmidt?" Donati asked.

"He's the right age," Bruno answered as they watched him enter the woman's residence.

The five feet ten inches tall man, who appeared to be in his mid-sixties and carried an extra fifteen pounds, all in the gut, had salt and paper hair cut close to the scalp because of several bald spots. He wore business-casual khaki pants and a long sleeve light blue shirt.

When Donais returned to the terrace restaurant, they looked at her photos and texted them to Acardi.

Forty-five minutes later, Acardi called Bruno.

"Although these photos weren't in our databases," he said, "the French had them in their system. The woman is Karin Schmidt, who became a French citizen while maintaining her German passport because France permits dual citizenship. The man is Ulrick Schmidt, also a dual citizen and the owner of the Peugeot."

"The next question we need to answer is whether he's enjoying retirement with his mother or returned after a day restoring artwork."

"How do you find out?" Acardi asked Bruno.

"We follow him and, if that doesn't lead anywhere, have a very personal conversation with Ulrick Schmidt."

"Be careful, Mauro, he's a French citizen and all you have on him is a supposition without facts."

"I know."

After the call ended, Bruno repeated his conversation with Acardi and said that Ulrick and his mother were likely in for the night and that they needed a good night's sleep and would meet at seven tomorrow morning. With everyone exhausted from stress and a lack of sleep, no one argued, and they went to their rooms.

Sunrise was at 6:47 am, and although the terrace restaurant opened at seven, everyone except Bruno was at their table several minutes after the sun announced its presence. He arrived five minutes later, wiping his hands with a paper towel from the men's room before putting the steak knife he'd taken the previous evening back on the table.

"I assume there's a story behind that knife," Hunkler said.

"Our plan is to follow Ulrick to his employer, assuming he has one, with one or more of us running to the minivan and following him."

Everyone agreed that was the plan.

"It's not going to work. When it was dark, I timed how long it would take to go from this table and receive our key from the valet, assuming he was at his post, and get to our car."

"How long did it take?" Hunkler asked.

"Too long. To race down two staircases and run up the gravel drive, which is on the opposite side of the hotel from the terrace, and hope the valet isn't parking another vehicle or otherwise occupied, seventy-five seconds."

"Schmidt would be long gone by then," Donati said.

"I decided to even the odds," Bruno continued, picking up the steak knife. "When he gets to his car, he's going to find he has a flat tire, giving us ample time to get to our vehicle and follow him."

"Smart," Hunkler said, "as long as he isn't running errands today, which is Saturday. We can only use this ruse once."

"We'll find out," Bruno said as the server approached their table to hand our menus.

At nine-thirty, an hour and a half after the others returned to their rooms, Hunkler was sipping a glass of Perrier at their terrace table when he saw Ulrick Schmidt leave the house. He called Bruno, afterward seeing Schmidt kick the offending tire and go into the trunk of his car to retrieve a spare. Not waiting to see his tire-changing skills, Hunkler went to the minivan where the rest of the team, having been called by Bruno, were waiting.

It took thirty-five minutes for Schmidt to change the tire, go back to the house and clean up, and return to his vehicle. When he finally drove away, he took a circuitous shortcut route to the motorway. Hunkler, experienced at tailing vehicles, kept his distance but had the Peugeot in sight most of the way. Forty-five minutes and eighteen miles later, they entered Saint-Jean-Cap-Ferrat, an exclusive community of sixteen hundred on the eastern side of the Ferrat Peninsula, the second most expensive residential real estate in the world next to Monaco.

Hunkler followed the Peugeot to the peninsula's tip, which ended at two massive, ten-foot-high black swing gates, each capped with a row of golden spear tips. They were connected to an equally high stone wall that surrounded the property. Outside and to the left of the gates was a stone-faced guardhouse with a large rectangular bulletproof window that allowed the two security personnel within to view approaching vehicles. Seeing the gates, the colonel quickly pulled the minivan to the side of the road a hundred yards from the guardhouse and beside the lush vegetation of another property, making it difficult to see.

They watched as Schmidt stopped his vehicle in front of the gates and rolled down his window so that security could verify he was the driver. No sooner did this happen than the gates swung open, allowing the Peugeot onto the palm-lined gravel drive that led to the mansion.

"It looks like we may have found the person we're looking for," Donais said.

"But how do we get inside? I'm betting this person has a boatload of money and corresponding influence, making it difficult for us to threaten them or bluff our way onto the estate," Bruno stated. "Now that we have a location, I'll call Acardi and see what he can tell us about the owner and this property. In the meantime, let's get out of here. A minivan parked alongside the road in this neighborhood isn't going to be inconspicuous. Let's return to the hotel and figure out our next move."

With everyone agreeing it was better not to press their luck, Hunkler made a U-turn and retraced his route to the highway. It was 11:10 am.

At six that evening, the team assembled in Bruno's room for an update from Acardi, who was on speakerphone.

"The thirty-five-acre Saint-Jean-Cap-Ferrat estate is owned by the Vogel family trust, with Reinhard Vogel as the trustee, and was purchased in nineteen fifty-five."

"It must be a large trust," Bruno commented.

"According to the town's taxing authority, the property is worth four hundred million dollars."

"How did the trust get its money?" Bruno continued.

"Let me give you Vogel's family history from the end of World War II, and you can draw your own conclusions," Acardi began. "Reinhard Vogel was born in Berlin in nineteen forty-four, the son of a Nazi SS officer who was killed a month before the fall of the city to the Allies. His father was believed to have been empowered by the Fuhrer to organize and implement the looting of art from homes, museums, and private collections in occupied lands. Vogel disbursed this plunder to salt mines, castles, and other secretive locations in Austria and Germany, most of which are believed to have been discovered."

"How much art are we talking about?" Donati asked.

"Six-hundred and fifty-thousand works, twenty percent of all the art in Europe, over one-hundred thousand of which have never been recovered," Milani answered.

"You know your numbers," Acardi complimented. "The Allies who entered Berlin never found a complete list of the looted art and antiquities, nor where it was hidden. What they learned came from the German soldiers who transported and stored the pieces. It's believed that many of these are in Swiss bank vaults, along with gold and jewels that could be quickly turned into cash."

"Vogel's father gives his wife the list of stolen art and antiquities and where they were kept. Following the war, she sells gold and jewels for cash and moves the stolen items to a central location in case others knew about these hiding places," Donais theorized.

"That's the prevailing theory, although no one has been able to prove it. Following the war," Acardi continued, "people in war-torn countries were trying to survive, and feeding and housing them was the priority of interim governments and their occupiers. Therefore, no one focused on Vogel's wife because she wasn't a war criminal or part of Hitler's government. Ten years later, she establishes a trust and purchases the largest estate in Saint-Jean-Cap-Ferrat for her and her son, Reinhard—an eighteen thousand square feet mansion."

"It must have driven the conspiracy theorists crazy that she had access to so much cash ten years after the war," Bruno said.

"It did, and several months after she bought the estate, the police raided it to search for stolen art and money. They found nothing. Following the raid, she began spreading money around, donating to local charities, government officials, and the campaigns of those who didn't care how she got wealthy but only wanted to be in office. With no evidence of wrongdoing and with the trust's philanthropic and political donations, no one bothered the mother or son again. She passed away in two thousand ten at ninety, which is when Reinhard became the successor trustee."

"What do we know about him?" Bruno asked.

"The trust owns a one hundred ten feet long boat, which is docked at the local marina, and a seventy-five million dollar Gulfstream G700, which he keeps at the Côte d'Azur Airport."

"Does he or his trust own any other residences?" Bruno continued.

"None that I could find. But I only have access to EU databases and not that of the Americans or any in South America or Asia," Acardi cautioned.

"Understood," Bruno said. "Now that we know a little more about the person who we assume is the collector. How do we get inside the mansion and find out if they have the Mona Lisa?"

Everyone was silent until Milani spoke up.

"The Vatican is similar in some ways to this estate," the curmudgeon said. "Other than those who work within, an invitation is required to get past security and enter the non-tourist areas. As we're unlikely to get an invite from Reinhard Vogel, we need to force the invitation."

"How do we do that?" Hunkler asked.

"By giving him a problem that only we can solve."

"Which is?"

Milani told him.

A little before seven that evening, Acardi phoned Lamberti with Milani's idea and Bruno's requests.

"Now that we know the probable location of the Mona Lisa and Vatican paintings, I'll set in motion what Milani is asking us to do while you arrange for everyone's return to Italy once the paintings are back in our possession," Lamberti said.

"That works. I was thinking of sending a boat to Saint-Jean-Cap-Ferrat so that Bruno and his team won't have to pass through customs and immigration when they leave because, for all anyone knows, they're cruising in French waters. Instead, it'll sail to Genoa, only a hundred and twenty miles away. We'll then fly the paintings and the team to Rome."

"That could work," Lamberti agreed. "Let's get started."

Once their conversation ended, Lamberti phoned Montanari and explained what she wanted and where it would happen.

"They engineer power grids to be impenetrable to hackers because they're a national security concern," the savant began. "In my previous profession, I avoided them because penetrating their firewalls was time-consuming, and these networks are monitored

24/7. If a grid shuts down, an alarm sounds, and someone in a control center will try to determine the cause of the failure. If they can't fix the problem, they'll dispatch a crew to the location."

"Can you take down the power at a specific residence so it can't be restored from the control center?" Lamberti asked, ignoring his monologue.

"Only if I'm in the system."

"That's what I need."

"Even if I do this, it's almost a given that they'll have a backup generator. I've never seen an estate this large that didn't," the reformed thief said.

Lamberti knew he was right because her mansion had a generator. "Can it be hacked and inactivated?" she asked.

"Most generators allow remote access through an app, which can be hacked. However, I'd need to know the brand of the generator."

"You'll have to get it on your own."

"The estate will have a company that services the unit. I'll get it from them."

"How long will you need?"

"Half a day to a day, depending on the complexities I encounter in finding the service company and hacking the app."

"That works."

"I assume you want the grid and generator to go down at the same time?"

"That's a must. Those inside the mansion need to be desperate for power and will do anything to get it back."

"I'll get started."

13

Montanari didn't know squat about power grid systems. Therefore, following his call with Lamberti, he spent several hours searching the internet and reading every snippet of information he could find on the methodology used by hackers to access power grids and, once inside, prevent the utility from regaining control until they released the system.

The savant began his hack of the Saint-Jean-Cap-Ferrat power grid by looking for job offers that the utility posted on the internet. Finding one, he used the same procedures he employed at the Louvre to breach their firewall and access the intranet.

The operations side of the network was "air-gapped" from the administrative section—an air gap meaning there's no connection between the two because they're digitally isolated. However, Montanari knew air gaps were a fallacy and that an experienced hacker understood all data resided within the same system. Therefore, there was always a pathway between them—if one could find it. Dusting off a program he'd used nearly a decade ago when he made his money as a hacker and thief; he modified his algorithm to employ the methodology used by others who'd successfully penetrated utilities and found the pathway.

Once the savant was on the operational side of the system, he inserted a crash override—malware that circumvented the utility's

Supervisory Control and Data Acquisition (SCADA) software and their Energy Management System (EMS), giving him hands-on-the-switches access. At 1:45 am, he conducted a test, briefly shutting down electricity to a residence. After verifying that he could turn off a user's power, he exited the system and focused his attention on his next problem, which was eliminating the estate's backup power—making the assumption the estate had a generator.

Finding the company which performed the periodic inspections that generators underwent took far more time than expected. Because he didn't know which company performed the work, he made a list of inspection contractors within a twenty-mile radius. There were eight. He then hacked their systems to see if Vogel's name or address was in their billing system, coming up empty. He expanded his search area to thirty miles and came away with three more generator service companies, eventually finding the estate's address in the billing system of the third company.

Once in the company's database, Montanari learned Vogel had a three hundred kVA backup generator—ten times the size found in a typical residence. This model was the most expensive and had what the industry called a cloud interface, meaning it could be remotely operated, which fit perfectly with the savant's plans in that it allowed him to access the unit at will.

It was four o'clock on Sunday morning when he called Lamberti and told her he had complete control over the estate's power.

The five were sitting at their terrace table when Acardi updated Bruno, telling him that Montanari had the power situation in hand and how his team and the art they were repatriating would leave the country. He then went over the specifics so there were no misunderstandings. Once the call ended, Bruno repeated what he'd been told to ensure everyone was on the same page.

"Montanari will cut the power to the estate and inactivate the backup generator. With the mansion dark, the outage will be reported to the utility, which will query their system and learn that no power is going to Vogel's residence. However, they won't be able to reestablish power because Montanari will have God-like control of their system. As this happens, we borrow one or more utility vehicles and enter the estate on the pretext of fixing the problem."

"Do we know where the utility vehicles are parked?" Donati asked.

"We passed them near the Rothschild Garden on our way to the estate," Hunkler responded. "The lot is gated but doesn't appear especially secure."

Donais said she also saw the lot.

"I can hotwire the vehicles, and we can be on our way in minutes. The open question is whether there's security," Hunkler added.

"I'm guessing there isn't," Donais said. "Thieves would want more than a work vehicle in this ritzy area."

Everyone agreed that made sense.

"That leaves the question of how to get IDs and the utility company uniforms to establish our creds with the estate guards," Bruno said.

"The vehicles will be an indirect verification that we're from the utility," Donais volunteered.

"Maybe. But our attire and appearance will be the problem," Donati added. "Look at us. We're older than the typical line worker. People our age would have seniority and occupy management positions, not responding to nighttime outages. The dottore looks like he should be chairman of the utility company."

"It's the hand we're dealt. We have to go with it," Hunkler said. "We can wear a hard hat to cover the gray hair, making our age less obvious, and the dottore can act as the onsite supervisor.

But I agree we must look the part by wearing the proper working attire or something close to it."

"Returning to our discussion of the estate," Bruno said, "we need a plausible explanation on why we're looking around the interior of the mansion rather than working outside to fix the problem.

"My father's home has a utility room in the basement," Donati said, Bruno and Donais knowing that the family's home was a ten thousand square feet mansion in Milan, where his father was an executive at Kering's Italian subsidiary. "If we lose power, we check for a tripped circuit breaker in one of the power panels in the utility room. A mansion this size will have multiple power panels. It's logical for a utility company to check them first."

"That makes sense, and it'll be our pretext to get inside," Bruno said. "However, because security will expect us to be French, Lisette will need to be the only one speaking with them."

"C'est une bonne idée," Donais said, drawing a laugh.

"Since there won't be any light, we'll need night vision goggles to search the mansion without being seen and two-way radios with a common frequency," Hunkler added. "We'll also need flashlights to complete our image of maintenance workers."

"Those are excellent suggestions," Bruno said. "Tomorrow, we'll go shopping."

"When do we breach the mansion?" Hunkler asked.

"Tomorrow night," Bruno answered.

"Once the painting is known to be missing, Vogel's security will come after us with a vengeance," Donati said. "The yacht had better be at the marina."

"We have enough to worry about without getting into Acardi's space. He's never let us down before. Let's hope that record continues."

With everyone acknowledging that tomorrow would be a long day, they retired for the evening.

The following morning, Bruno called Acardi, and they decided that 10:00 pm was the optimum time to cut the estate's power, the darkness and lateness of the day working in their favor.

Following the call, Bruno searched the internet for area stores that had what they needed, discovering it was the norm in France that businesses were closed on Sundays. Unable to get what they needed for the rouse, he called Acardi and told him they had to move everything back by a day.

The night vision goggles were the hardest to find, Hunkler discovering that the only store in the area that sold them was in Provence—a two-hour drive from Saint-Paul-de-Vence. The good news was that it also had two-way radios in inventory, making it one-stop shopping. After purchasing the items, they walked to a nearby business that had work clothes, hard hats, heavy-duty flashlights, and other items used by maintenance workers, returning to their hotel at three.

Once they dropped off the purchases in their rooms, they went to the terrace for a bite, only to discover a family was sitting at their usual table. Bruno selected another in the opposite corner. They ordered, and once it came and the server left, he summarized everyone's responsibilities, setting eight-thirty as the time they'd assemble at the minivan.

Hunkler was ex-military, Bruno and Donati ex-police officers, and Donais was a private investigator. All were accustomed to pre-operation tension. Milani wasn't and looked as nervous as a novice trying to climb Mount Everest. Seeing this, Bruno told a couple of funny stories about some of the raids he participated in, causing everyone to laugh. Donais, seeing what Bruno was doing, had her own stories, followed by those of Donati and Hunkler, who used the term FUBAR, which was new to Milani and caused him to roar with laughter when the colonel told him it was military jargon and an abbreviation for fucked up beyond all recognition. When they left the table, the team was relaxed and focused on what they needed to do.

It was dark when they assembled at the vehicle, with Hunkler again being the driver. Once out of sight of the hotel and surrounding residences, he pulled to the side of the road where each donned a thick work jumpsuit over their clothing, replaced their shoes with boots, and put on a hard hat. Fifteen minutes later, they were on their way to Saint-Jean-Cap-Ferrat.

"Let's go by the marina and see if our yacht is there," Bruno said, everyone agreeing that taking its presence for granted wouldn't be a good idea."

"What was the name of the boat that Acardi gave you?" Donais asked Bruno.

"*Princess*," he replied.

Hunkler entered the marina, which had five hundred eighty-one moorings and dozens of mega yachts. They spotted the one hundred eighty feet long *Princess* to the left of the entrance, its name brightly illuminated on the hull.

"Let's get to work," Bruno said, seeing the smiles on everyone's faces.

At nine forty-five, they arrived at the utility's administrative building—a single-story structure made from Kolumba bricks that were dark maroon. Beside it was a dimly lit gravel parking lot with three utility trucks sitting side-by-side. Hunkler stepped out of the minivan with bolt cutters, sheared the lock, and pushed back the gate. Going to the first truck, he opened the driver's door and pulled down the sun visor—the vehicle's keys dropping onto the seat.

"How did you know the truck would be unlocked and the keys inside?" Bruno asked in astonishment.

"I assumed they might do the same as the Vatican does with its emergency response vehicles. In a crisis, where seconds count, it takes time to retrieve the keys from a central location and get them to the vehicle. This way, all that's needed is a key to the gate."

"That's good thinking. I'll park the minivan in the parking lot of one of the shops down the street," Bruno said. "You and Donais will be in the lead truck, Donati and Milani in another, and I'll be in the last," he said, loud enough for everyone to hear.

"We're taking all the trucks?" Donati asked.

"We need to. This station is close to the estate. When someone from the mansion calls the utility and says their power is out, they'll dispatch one of these trucks. If a real utility crew gets to the estate while we're there, security will know we're imposters, and we may not leave the mansion alive. If these vehicles aren't here, they'll have to dispatch one from a facility that's further away."

"Good thinking."

"I'll park the minivan in a lot up the street and be back in ten," Bruno said.

The estate's primary power and backup generator went offline at precisely ten o'clock, the five approaching the estate in their utility vehicles several minutes later. Upon seeing the mansion, Hunkler pulled to the side of the road and turned off his engine, the other vehicles parking behind it. Everyone then exited their trucks and assembled around the lead vehicle, knowing they had a huge problem.

"Why isn't the power cut?" Bruno asked, looking at his watch and seeing it was six past the hour. Because it was a rhetorical question, he didn't expect a response and called Acardi, explaining their predicament.

"I was told utility and generator power were inoperative. Let me conference Montanari and Lamberti into the call," he said.

When the savant answered, with Lamberti on the line, Bruno explained that lights were on throughout the estate.

"I inactivated the utility's breaker to the estate and gave a shutdown command to the generator, commands only I can override," Montanari answered as he looked at his computer screen and verified the shutdowns. "If the estate has power, it's because they have another generator, which is difficult to understand because I checked every service company within a thirty-mile radius of the mansion. Only one billed that address."

"This plan isn't going to work," Lamberti said, pulling the plug on the operation. "Return the vehicles to the utility yard before they figure out they've been stolen and return to the hotel," she said. "We'll talk then."

It was eleven-thirty when the five walked onto the terrace of the Colombe d'Or Hotel. Although the restaurant had technically closed thirty minutes earlier, guests were still dining at several tables and enjoying the evening air. The attentive and amiable staff, knowing Bruno and his group were hotel guests, brought cold bottles of Acqua Panna water to their table and explained that the kitchen had closed for the day. Bruno asked the server to bring two bottles of local red wine.

"It's almost Tuesday morning. On Sunday, the Mona Lisa is scheduled to be returned to the Louvre Paris," Bruno began. "If we can't cut power to the other generator, we need to find another way to retrieve the three paintings."

"Ulrick Schmidt has access to the mansion," Donais said. "He could be our ticket to get inside."

"Even if we could convince him to cooperate, we need a plausible reason the five of us must accompany him—one that Vogel and the guards will buy. Even then, we'll be closely watched, giving us little chance of taking the Mona Lisa and two Vatican paintings with us as parting gifts," Donati quipped.

"What about the police receiving an anonymous tip that Vogel is hiding stolen works of art?" Milani asked.

"Setting aside Vogel's connections and influence, the local police will not raid a mansion in Saint-Jean-Cap-Ferrat based on a tip that sounds incredulous on its face," Hunkler stated. "If someone made a similar call to the Vatican without some measure of proof, I'd discount it as a crank call."

"Even if the police showed up, searched the mansion, and found the stolen art, they're not going to give us the paintings under the table so we can return them. The Mona Lisa belongs to the French people. There will be enormous fanfare around its recovery with recriminations made against the Vatican for losing it and putting a fake in its place," Donais stated.

Milani agreed.

"Maybe the authorities aren't a bad alternative," Bruno said.

"Haven't you been listening?" Donati asked.

"Not the local police, another law enforcement agency," Bruno said, tapping a business card on the table.

The five returned to their rooms at one in the morning, after which Bruno called Acardi and Lamberti and told them what he intended to do.

"This will blow up in your face if you misjudge either person," Acardi warned.

"We're out of options. It's this, or the French have a meltdown on Sunday when we hand them back a reproduction of the most famous painting in the world."

"Tread cautiously," Lamberti said, tacitly giving her approval. "As you know, our government requires the support of both houses of Parliament. Even though the president has overriding support in the Senate of the Republic, he has only the narrowest margin in the Chamber of Deputies. If this goes wrong, it could bring down the government with a vote of no confidence."

Bruno said he knew the consequences and would throw his body on the grenade caused by his actions to protect her and the president.

"You won't have to," Lamberti replied. "It'll be a large grenade, and the shrapnel will take out all of us."

Bruno called Bence at eight that morning, asking if he'd come to the Colombe d'Or Hotel for coffee because he needed that favor. The captain said he'd come right over and walked onto the terrace at ten past nine wearing his usual work attire: a suit and tie. Bruno introduced Hunkler by name, the only member of the five who Bence hadn't met.

The captain sat in the chair that was left vacant for him between Bruno and Donati and ordered a cup of espresso from the server, who saw him join the five. Various pastries were on the table, and Bence helped himself to a croissant.

"Thank you for coming, captain," Bruno began. "Let me tell you why we're here and the favor I need. We may also be able to return the favor by apprehending an international art thief who's living in Saint-Jean-Cap-Ferrat."

"That sounds intriguing, but understand I work for the Directorate-General of Customs and Indirect Taxes, which means that unless we're talking about smuggling, counterfeit money, or border security, the agency you should be speaking with is the gendarmerie. They have law enforcement responsibilities in small towns and rural areas under twenty thousand inhabitants. In France, law enforcement agencies tend to be very territorial," Bence said before taking a large bite of his croissant.

"We're talking about stolen art that's been smuggled into the country."

"I'm interested," Bence stated, sipping the espresso the server had placed in front of him."

Bruno began by giving the team's backgrounds before summarizing the trail that led them to Karin and Ulrick Schmidt and Reinhard Vogel, and the suspected sale of masterpieces to him. The Mona Lisa wasn't mentioned.

Bence listened intently to Bruno's fifteen-minute explanation, polishing off another croissant and a second cup of espresso during that time. "Reading between the lines and judging from the call I received at the airport to release you, I'd say the Italian government is involved in your efforts. Why are they interested in a suspected art thief living in France? If they believe this thief has paintings they've smuggled from Italy, a call between presidents could apprehend this person."

"We'd like to surprise them and raid his residence."

"That's a serious matter. I'm not sure that's possible."

Bruno momentarily looked at Bence without speaking, realizing the captain believed he was holding something back and needed the entire story. "That call between governments can't be made because the painting we believe Vogel has in his possession isn't known to be missing because a forgery has been put in its place. The painting belongs to France, and my government is responsible for it."

"Can I know the name of the painting?"

"The Mona Lisa," Bruno said after briefly hesitating, deciding to trust Bence.

"The one on display at the Vatican is a forgery?"

Milani interrupted, saying that it was and that the two Vatican paintings on loan to the Louvre were also forgeries and believed to be in Vogel's possession.

"I understand the Mona Lisa will be returned to the Louvre this Sunday."

"Now you know our problem."

"As an ex-law enforcement officer," Bence said to Bruno in a sympathetic voice, "you realize you have no proof for any of the allegations you've made against Vogel."

"I believe that Ulrick Schmidt could verify those allegations."

"Let me explain French law."

"Lisette Donais gave us a brief explanation. She was an investigator for a Paris attorney before becoming our partner," Bruno said.

"With all respect to your lovely partner, let me review it again so we're on the same page. As she undoubtedly told you, unlike Italy, France doesn't use search warrants. If a crime is in process, I have the right to search the premises. If an official investigation has been opened, I can conduct a search at any time except between nine pm and six am unless we're talking about organized crime or terrorism, in which case the time restriction doesn't apply. If I'm in the preliminary stages of an investigation trying to gather enough credible information for it to become official, then I can only search with the owner's approval. Therefore, the only way to conduct the search we're discussing is to formally open an investigation."

"How is that done?" Hunkler asked.

"If it's a criminal circumstance, an investigating judge initiates the matter and gathers evidence to see if a crime has been committed. If they determine it has, they refer the matter to the trial court."

"That's not going to work in this situation," Bruno said. "Any suggestions?"

"Lean on Ulrick Schmidt and get a statement from him on Vogel's possession of the stolen art."

"Leaning on him may be a problem because we have no proof that he's done anything wrong. He could refuse to speak with us without something to hold over him. If he warns Vogel, we'll never recover the Mona Lisa," Bruno responded.

"I could give him civil immunity, a contract between the government and a witness in exchange for their testimony."

"That may work."

"The offer of immunity and a threat from me will carry weight. A group of Italians threatening a French citizen with wild unsubstantiated accusations, which he'll deny, would likely result in him calling the police and having you thrown out of his house, creating a paper trail I'm sure your government would like to avoid. This is a French matter. I'll tell him the downside of non-cooperation, with the immunity giving him a way to maintain his lifestyle and freedom in exchange for what he knows. However, while I can convert what he tells me into an official investigation, it'll take time. Therefore, I'd like to make two suggestions."

"As I have two toes over the edge of a cliff with the wind at my back, please," Bruno said, bringing a smile to the captain's face.

"Use Schmidt to learn whether the stolen paintings, including the Mona Lisa and those from the Vatican, are at Vogel's mansion."

"And second?"

"He believes that some of the containers arriving at the mansion are too heavy to contain art and instead believes that weapons are inside."

"That bypasses the need for an investigation," Bruno said.

"And allows me to search Vogel's estate without warning, using the five of you as experts to identify the stolen art believed to be inside."

"That's stretching the rubber band to its limit. Will your boss buy that story and let you invade a home in the richest enclave in France occupied by a billionaire who undoubtedly has friends in high places?"

"No. But when terrorist activity is suspected, I'm given broad authority to act quickly and unilaterally."

"How broad?"

"I'll let you know the day after the raid when you'll either address me as captain or lieutenant."

At seven that evening, Bence joined Bruno and the rest of the team in front of the hotel as they walked to Schmidt's home. It was agreed that he would take the lead—flashing his credentials to enter the residence and scaring Ulrick into telling what he knew about the stolen paintings. Bence would also lead him to say that Vogel might be a closet terrorist smuggling arms in containers marked as art. To effectuate this voluntary outpouring of information, he'd brought a signed civil immunity contract stamped with the seal of the Directorate-General of Customs and Indirect Taxes.

Bence pounded on the door, and Ulrick Schmidt answered seconds later. The captain introduced himself, showed his badge, and asked if they could enter.

"What's this about?" Schmidt asked.

"Illegal art and terrorism. If you'd rather discuss that elsewhere, I can take you to the station in the back of my police vehicle," he bluffed. "But I'm sure that would create rumors with your neighbors."

Ulrick reluctantly invited them inside and directed the six to a sitting room where his mother was having an apéritif. Another glass on the small table next to her indicated her son had been seated in the chair beside it when Bence knocked. The startled mother asked her son in German what was happening. He told her what Bence had said.

Ulrick directed everyone to two couches. Bruno, Donati, and Hunkler elected to stand.

"Do you speak English?" Bence asked, knowing that only Donais would understand their conversation if it continued in French.

"Yes, but I'm not fluent," Ulrick answered.

"Neither am I," Bence replied. "Let me get to the point by telling you that Reinhard Vogel is under investigation for receiving stolen art. Do you know anything about this?"

Ulrick's mother, who also understood English, said something to him in German.

"I don't know a Reinhard Vogel," Ulrick said immediately afterward.

"That's odd, because I saw you driving into his compound in Saint-Jean-Cap-Ferrat."

"You've been following me?"

Bence ignored the question. "We could go back and forth all day with you professing to have memory lapses or outright lying to my questions. But I should warn you that besides receiving stolen art, I suspect Vogel is involved with terrorists. That presumption gives me the right to detain and question you, freeze your bank accounts, put a lien on this residence so it can't be sold, impound your vehicle, and make your life shit until I feel I'm getting the truth. I'm not going to waste time. If you don't get rid of your memory lapse in the next thirty seconds, I will place you in handcuffs, parade you down the street to my vehicle, and put you in an interrogation room long enough for you to call it your second home."

Ulrick got the point.

"What do you want to know?" he asked, the resignation that he had to answer Bence's questions evident in his voice.

"What do you do for Vogel?"

"I maintain and restore the paintings in his collection—at least the paintings I see."

"Does that collection include stolen art?"

Ulrick hesitated for a moment. "It's mostly stolen art," he answered.

"How many paintings does he have?"

"Twelve thousand two hundred and twenty-three paintings, only a fraction of which need restoration."

"He has over twelve thousand stolen paintings?"

"Some are purchased on the black market; others are bought anonymously at auction by phone. However, most of his works are stolen. That's a complicated story."

"What's complicated about it?"

"I'll get to that later."

Although Bruno and his team had questions, they didn't want to interrupt Bence, who was getting what they needed from Ulrick.

"These paintings must occupy every square inch of wall in the mansion."

"It's too difficult to control the temperature and humidity in a mansion that's more than a century old, especially living near the sea. He displays his art in a fifty-seven thousand square feet underground gallery."

"That's over three times the size of his mansion," Bence exclaimed.

"Not all that space is for displaying art. Behind a soundproof partition are environmental control equipment and natural gas generators large enough to power the gallery, mansion, and estate grounds. The outside generator is large enough to service the mansion and grounds if power is lost. If it fails, the underground generators can handle the load."

"Why two generators?"

"Paranoia that the backup generator might fail and there would be an extended power outage. The second generator is his insurance policy that the environmental conditions in the gallery will remain constant. This extends the life of a painting and lessens the need for restoration. When you have as much money as Vogel, it's an insignificant expenditure."

"How do we get into the gallery?" Bence asked.

"Without Reinhard Vogel's cooperation, it's impossible."

"Explain impossible."

"The stairway to the gallery is beyond a wood-paneled heavy steel door in his library. Entry requires his retinal and hand scan and a twelve number-letter-symbol passcode that changes daily," Schmidt said.

"He seems obsessed with security, which begs the question of how you know all this."

"I see the security procedures when he leads me into his gallery. Herr Vogel is also a narcissist, bragging about everything. He once told me he has a safe room, but I couldn't tell you where it is."

"You said most of his works are stolen and that it was a complicated story you'd explain later. Now is the time," Bence stated.

"Thievery runs in the family. Most of his paintings come from the Nazi's highly organized and systematic plunder of art during World War II. His father was placed in charge of this effort by Hitler and answered only to him, hiding the stolen art in secure locations in Germany and Austria and protecting it from the Allies' bombing raids. Along with stolen art, Hitler trusted him with hiding gold, silver, and precious jewels."

"Since his father died at the war's end, he must have given the ledgers listing what was stolen and where it was hidden to his wife."

"That would be the logical assumption given his current wealth."

"Most people don't share these dark secrets."

"Being a narcissist and a heavy drinker of schnapps is a bad combination. I've learned a lot in my almost twenty-eight years working for him."

"Why roll over on him now?"

"At sixty-three, I'm too old to go to jail. Any sentence I receive would effectively incarcerate me for life. Who will take care of my mother when I'm sent away?"

"This may ease those concerns," Bence said, taking two folded immunity letters from his inside jacket pocket and handing them to Ulrick, who took his time reading the document with his mother. "It says that I suspect Reinhard Vogel of being involved in terrorist activities because the heavy containers marked as art and smuggled onto his estate may be weapons."

"The raid of Vogel's estate doesn't happen unless he's believed to be involved, even tangentially, in terrorist activities. They'll come a time when you'll be asked that question under oath. Don't sign this document if you have a problem saying that."

"I can say that the thought occurred to me that there could be weapons, bombs, or explosive materials in the containers that came to the estate because Herr Vogel is not a supporter of the current government and sometimes has extreme political views."

"You also told me," Karin Schmidt added, "that your employer often expressed sympathy for the plight of those fighting Westerners in the Middle East and believed that he was sympathetic to their cause."

After his mother's comments and a nod from her, he signed both sets of immunity agreements, keeping one and returning the other to the captain.

"Now that this is out of the way, let's go back to something you said earlier about maintaining the paintings in his collection that you see. Are there paintings that are hidden from you?"

"There's a section of the gallery that has a cipher entry. I get a glimpse inside now and then when Vogel enters—enough to see that the art displayed on the walls are very famous paintings."

"Why are they in a protected room within a protected space? Second, why aren't you allowed to see them? You've seen thousands of his stolen paintings?"

"Because I don't believe he wants anyone to know he has them, not even me. They're too toxic. If their location were revealed, several nations would be all over the French government for their return."

"How did you see them?"

"When he opened the door to the room, I saw some of them displayed on the far wall."

"Name one or two."

"Raphael's Portrait of a Young Man, which the Nazis stole in Poland in nineteen thirty-nine, and Vincent Van Gogh's Painter on the Road to Tarascon, which is believed to have been destroyed when the allies bombed Magdeburg, Germany, and destroyed the Kaiser-Friedrich Museum, where the painting was displayed. Obviously, Vogel's father had removed the painting before that."

"How much are they worth?"

"Whatever a motivated buyer will pay. Raphael's painting should sell for one hundred million dollars plus, and Van Gogh's for sixty or seventy, possibly higher, given its history."

"The paintings we're looking for could be in that space."

"If they're especially valuable, and he doesn't want anyone but him to see them, they're there."

"Do you have any questions?" Bence asked Bruno.

"Have you seen containers from Museum Shipping being brought inside the room?"

"Sometimes."

"When was the last time?"

"About a week ago."

"Schmidt is reputed to be seventy-nine years old and without heirs. Why does he still collect them without someone to carry on his legacy?"

"Who told you he didn't have an heir? Vogel married in his forties and had a son born in the mansion. You couldn't find anything on him because the family doctor didn't put the father or mother on the birth certificate."

"Effectively making him an orphan able to create his own identity," Donati said.

"What do you know about him?" Bruno continued.

"He's an attorney."

"What's their name?"

"His first name is Friedrich, which is how Vogel addresses him. I assume his surname is Vogel."

"I doubt it," Bruno said.

"Why?"

"Because nearly every assumption we've made has been wrong."

15

The raid on Vogel's estate took place three days after the meeting with Schmidt, enough time to get the necessary approvals from those up the chain of command from Bence to conduct the raid under the nation's terrorist laws and organize the assault. It began with clockwise precision at 6:00 am when five police cruisers, followed by a minivan, pulled beside the guardhouse and ordered the two security personnel inside to open the gates. At the same time, four additional cruisers blocked the road on both sides of the estate.

Once the gates opened, the police cruisers raced to the front of the mansion. The security staff, seeing what was happening on the security cameras and not wanting to be drawn into a conflict with the police, opened the door and stood aside as the officers entered.

Asked by Bence for Vogel's location, one of the guards offered to escort him to the septuagenarian's bedroom, which was on the other side of the mansion.

"Find out where the library is and wait for me there while I get Vogel," Bence told Bruno.

The captain, accompanied by three officers, followed the guard to Vogel's bedroom, where Bence woke the septuagenarian out of a deep sleep, flashed his badge, threw back his sheet and comforter, and dragged him to his feet. Vogel, who was six feet tall, slender, had thinning gray hair, and wore dark blue silk pajamas, groggily slid his feet into his slippers.

Although Vogel was old, Bence hadn't expected his face to be nearly skeletal, nor that he'd have extensive bruising on both hands and feet.

"What are you doing in my home?" Vogel demanded.

Bence told him they'd received information that he was aiding terrorists, and the police were going to search the mansion.

"That's absurd. Get out of my house," he demanded in a hoarse voice that was barely audible. "You know French law. You need my permission."

"Not if I have a reasonable suspicion that you're assisting terrorists. Take me to your library," Bence said, handing the septuagenarian his robe and cane beside the bed.

The library was a thirty by thirty feet room with a ten feet high coffered ceiling, every square inch of which was covered with golden brown Bocote wood from the West Indies, one of the most expensive woods in the world. Two couches and several club chairs covered in dark brown leather were situated throughout the room.

While Bence told Vogel to remain where he was, three police officers searched the library, confiscating three handguns and a knife from various drawers.

"You have a choice Bence said to the septuagenarian once the officers finished. "You can open the door to your gallery or, to get inside, I'll tear apart what looks to be a very expensive library with heavy equipment."

When Vogel stepped toward the bookcase to his left, Bence grabbed his left arm. "Slowly," the captain cautioned.

The septuagenarian pulled a thick book on the shelf, after which a wooden panel slid to the side, exposing retinal and hand scanners and a keypad. "I'll need my phone for the current passcode," he said.

Bence, who'd taken his iPhone off the nightstand and pocketed it before they left the bedroom, handed it to him. Vogel got the passcode and went through the security procedures, after which an entry portal opened. The septuagenarian led the way, followed by the captain and the three officers, with Bruno and his team bringing up the rear. Beyond the portal was a wide, descending staircase with high ceilings, which ended in a well-lit fifty thousand square feet room.

"I think Schmidt was off on his painting count," Benco said, seeing that approximately two-thirds of the wall space was devoid of art. The cipher-protected room was to his right, just as Ulrick had described. However, the door was open, and no works of art were visible. A wave of nausea coursed through his body, and he did all he could to keep from vomiting.

Milani left the group and began examining the pieces of art which hung on the walls. Included among them were the paintings that Edward Stanley sold Vogel.

"You have a magnificent collection," Milani said. "I recall some of these were auctioned to anonymous buyers."

"Why such a large space for relatively few paintings?" Donais asked the septuagenarian in French.

Vogel didn't reply. Instead, he turned to Bence. "As you can see, captain, there are no terrorists or items used by them, nor stolen paintings, which I assume is the reason for this intrusion. If you and your officers are finished, leave the estate. I'll speak with my attorney and call several government officials, asking why this raid was sanctioned."

Bence had nothing further to say and apologized for the inconvenience. Speaking into the police radio he carried in his left hand, he told the assault group to leave the estate.

"Schmidt warned him," Bruno told Bence as they walked to their vehicles.

"I agree that's the only way he could have known since I don't believe the leak came from law enforcement or government officials. At least, I hope not. Why would Schmidt do it?"

"Because it wouldn't violate his immunity deal. He told us his suspicions and observations and, at our urging, included innuendos on terrorist activity so we could conduct the raid. Legally, he satisfied the conditions of his immunity agreement, meaning we can't come after him. He then tells Vogel about our planned intrusion, reaffirming his loyalty. Schmidt believes this will ensure his and his mother's safety because he saved Vogel's hide. However, he didn't think this through because the immunity we granted Schmidt only applies to France and not other countries where art was stolen. Vogel will figure this out and, in the near future, he'll need another restoration specialist."

"We had the estate under surveillance for the three days it took us to get the needed approvals and to organize the raid. How could he move so much art in such a short period? And how did he get it past us?"

"Good questions," Bruno said. "I'm sorry that I got you into this mess."

"Don't be. After seeing the empty wall space and the separate enclosure devoid of a single painting, I know he's your art thief. I don't know how to help you prove it, given every French law enforcement function will have a hands-off policy on him. If I remember correctly, you have forty-eight hours to find and return the Mona Lisa to the Vatican. What are you going to do?"

"That's a good question."

"They're gone," Vogel told Friedrich Becker. "Come over," he said in a raspy voice. His son, who used his mother's maiden name throughout life to make it difficult to associate him with his father and grandparents, replied that he'd drive over.

When it was listed for sale, Vogel bought the adjacent residence for him, afterward constructing a brick-lined tunnel between the mansions. Because both properties were large, they traversed the tunnel with golf carts, using them to transport the art between mansions.

They were boxed in one of two types of containers at his son's home, after which they were tagged and loaded onto an eighteen-wheeler for transport to the Charles de Gaulle Airport. Because the movement of the art outpaced the packing and shipping, numerous paintings clogged Becker's end of the tunnel. Therefore, the only way that he could get to his father's house was to drive.

The son was a younger version of his father. He stood six feet one inch tall, had a slender physique, and had black hair starting to gray. He entered the library and joined his father on the brown leather couch in the center of the room.

"I want you to start lawsuits this morning against the police, the government agency charged with their supervision, and Captain Bence. That will keep them away from here until we pack and transport the rest of the art."

"I can do that," the son replied.

"Are we on schedule?"

"We're slightly ahead. The trucks have brought in forty feet long climate-controlled maritime containers and wooden and multi-layered cardboard boxes faster than expected."

"Do we have enough? Some paintings will occupy an entire container or box."

"Marseille has a warehouse full of them and hundreds of environmentally controlled units designed to transport art, paper goods, and other temperature and humidity-sensitive items. We didn't put a dent in their supply."

"Well done," Vogel said, trusting the intricacies of the move to his son because, as an attorney, he was detail-oriented and took nothing for granted.

"The containers are stored in a bonded warehouse at the Charles de Gaulle Airport until loaded on the aircraft. The last paintings will be out of the tunnel and into their containers early this afternoon and leave my home for the airport around three."

"Have a tag and seal been affixed to every container?"

"Each one," Becker verified.

"Excellent, now sue the pants off everyone who violated my home."

"Do you believe the paintings were there?" Lamberti asked Bruno.

"The wall space was large enough to display the twelve thousand plus paintings that Schmidt told us were in Vogel's gallery. Milani pointed out that there were thousands of Ryman hangers at various heights on the wall, which he said are used by most major museums and galleries to hang art."

"Moving thousands of paintings from the estate would take days and require large transport vehicles. It couldn't have gone unnoticed with Bence's stakeout of the estate," Acardi said.

"That's if the main gate to the estate was the only way on or off the property," Bruno cautioned. "Bence's raid focused on finding the Mona Lisa and not seeing if there was another way to get off the property."

"Vogel's property is too large for a single police vehicle to cover," Acardi said.

"The main road ends at the estate's gates. If that's all that's being staked out, seeing the other three sides of the property is impossible. On the way there, we passed four or five feeder streets to smaller estates, but you can't see them if you're watching Vogel's gates," Bruno stated.

"Could Vogel's estate connect to one of those streets?" Acardi questioned.

"It's doubtful. When I drove through the area, I saw every homestead has hedges or walls around it, which gives one a good idea of the size of the estate. I didn't see a street or road that pierced the boundary of these homesteads or Vogels other than the street or road leading to its entrance. That said, a vehicle, even a massive one, could leave any of these mansions and get to the main highway unseen by the stakeout team."

"Meaning that if Vogel's property connects to one of these estates, he could have taken the art there once Schmidt warned him," Lamberti said.

"That's my belief," Bruno stated."

"That puts us in a difficult position because there's no way you or the police are getting back onto his property to find that connection. Let's hope the attorney keeps you and your team out of the fallout that's sure to come because, if he doesn't, it will be difficult to explain why you were there," Lamberti said.

"Vogel's attorney," Bruno whispered to himself, but loud enough for Lamberti and Acardi to hear.

"What about him?" Lamberti asked.

Bruno explained.

Friedrich Becker filed the lawsuit at 11:00 am, four hours before the last shipment of containers left for the Charles de Gaulle Airport. The complaint named Bence; the Directorate-General of Customs and Indirect Taxes; its supervisory agency, the Ministry for the Budget, Public Accounts and the Civil Service; and their supervisory agency, the Ministry of the Economy, Industry, and Employment. Bence, who received a verbal proctology exam from his superior, was suspended and told not to set foot in Saint-Jean-Cap-Ferrat. If there was any good news, it was that the complaint didn't mention Bruno or anyone on his team.

After calling Bence and learning of his suspension, Bruno invited him to their table on the terrace. The captain arrived at one that afternoon wearing civilian clothes and appearing haggard.

"You look like you've been through the wringer," Bruno said.

"Remember when I said that if this goes wrong the next time we speak, I might be a lieutenant?"

"I remember," Bruno acknowledged, his voice reflecting his guilt for dragging Bence into this.

"That might be wishful thinking. An official at the ministry in Paris, which oversees law enforcement, told my supervisor they're offering to fire me in return for the attorney dismissing the lawsuit. Even if Vogel's attorney doesn't accept it, that they proposed my termination says I'm history no matter the outcome."

"That's only the outcome if we can't link Vogel to the theft of the Mona Lisa or the paintings that Schmidt said were in his possession," Hunkler said.

"How would we do that since the paintings weren't on his property?" Bence asked.

"Vogel couldn't have moved that quantity of art in such a short time unless he'd previously planned for something like this and had a way to move it to a secure and undiscoverable location," Bruno said. "Where's his son's office, and where does he live?"

"I don't know," Bence confessed.

"Since he's the attorney, it should be on the complaint," Donati volunteered.

Bence called a law enforcement friend, who gave the address to him. After writing it down, he gave the paper to Donais, who looked at Google.

"How far is Vogel's house from his son's office?" Bruno asked.

Donais saw the red dot on her screen was the property next to Vogel's estate. "The address on the complaint is the property next to his father's estate. It appears he works from his home," she said.

"And his father is probably his only client," Hunkler added.

"That proximity might explain where the art went," Donati said. "The question is whether the paintings are still at his son's house or at another location."

"It doesn't matter. There's no way the police will search the residence of the attorney who filed Vogel's lawsuit against us," Bence stated.

"You're probably right," Bruno conceded, "but wouldn't you like to know what Vogel did with the art and turn the tables on him?"

"I would," Bence admitted.

"What are you doing the rest of the day?"

"Waiting to be fired. Why?"

"I have a plan."

"I hope it's better than your last one," Bence replied. "What is it?"

Bruno told him, with the others at the table hearing it for the first time.

16

Hunkler parked the minivan thirty yards from the gate to Becker's home, behind one of the thick-trunked fifty-foot-tall trees that lined the street. Bence, who was allowed to keep his police vehicle until a final decision on his future was rendered, was in his vehicle with Donati. They were behind a similar tree twenty-five yards on the opposite side of the gate from Hunkler.

Bruno's plan was to monitor Becker's home, believing Vogel had moved his illicit art there and that he'd either return it to the estate or send it somewhere he thought it would be safe from prying eyes. Bruno was counting on it being the latter, betting that Vogel would no longer consider the elaborate gallery he'd created secure because its existence was now known to outsiders. Since transport vehicles would be needed to move that large a quantity of art, Bruno believed they could follow the transports from Becker's home to Vogel's new hiding place.

That theory turned out to be correct. Twenty minutes after they began their surveillance, the gate opened, and an eighteen-wheeler left the residence and turned toward the minivan. Hunkler followed moments later, leaving a healthy distance between the minivan and the truck, with Bence's vehicle ten yards behind.

The truck driver wasted no time getting to the highway and taking the fork that led to Nice, eventually entering the A8 expressway toward Marseille before transitioning to the A7.

"Where does this expressway end?" Bruno asked Donais, who lived most of her life in France and was familiar with the highway system.

"The A7 ends in Lyon but connects with the A6, which ends in Paris."

"Either city is bad because we only have a quarter of a tank of gas, and we haven't passed any gas stations," Hunkler said.

"The government tries to keep the expressway visually pristine. We'll need to get off at one of the exits and refuel in an adjoining town, which is generally five to fifteen minutes from the expressway," Donais volunteered.

"Let me call Bence and see how much fuel he has. Maybe he can follow the truck while we get gas," Bruno said, discovering the police vehicle's gage was also registering a quarter of a tank.

"If it takes fifteen minutes to get to the gas station and five minutes to refuel, we'll be thirty-five minutes behind the truck. That means it'll be too far ahead to catch, and we won't know if it went to Lyon, Paris, or a town along the way," Hunkler said.

"It's six o'clock Friday night, and the Mona Lisa is scheduled to leave the Vatican on Sunday. We need to figure out something," Milani said.

"We do have an option, but Bence isn't going to like it," Bruno volunteered.

"He won't be surprised if it's coming from you," Hunkler stated.

Bruno's idea was to use the police car's flashing lights and siren to direct the truck to the side of the road and tell the driver to open the cargo compartment doors so they look inside and, if what they suspected was correct, find out where the driver was going.

"I shouldn't listen to you," Bence said when Bruno called, "but there's no other way to prove the paintings are on the truck and that Vogel's guilty of art theft, both of which are necessary to resurrect my career."

"And if they're not in the truck?"

"My pension is gone, and if I'm not arrested for representing myself as a law enforcement officer, even though I'm on suspension, I can start my career as a rent-a-cop tomorrow morning."

"What do you want to do? Losing your pension is serious," Bruno sympathized.

"So is losing my reputation," Bence responded and, after ending the call, switched on his vehicle's lights and siren, passed the minivan, and closed the distance to the truck.

The driver of the eighteen-wheeler didn't know what he'd done wrong. He'd kept his speed five miles per hour below the posted limit and signaled when he changed lanes. Confused, he pulled to the side of the road, seeing the police vehicle stop behind him with a minivan five yards to its rear.

Bence walked to the minivan and, after telling everyone to remain inside while he spoke with the driver, went to the truck and asked him to step out of the cab with his operator's license, vehicle documents, proof of insurance, and bill of lading.

"Can I see your badge?" the driver asked, noticing that Bence was in a suit and tie.

"You can see it at the station after I arrest you for not giving me what I asked for," Bence responded, unable to produce his badge because it was confiscated when he was suspended. "It's Friday night. You should be in court sometime on Monday for the bail hearing. In the meantime, I'll confiscate and search your truck. You can get it from the impound yard when the judge cuts you loose, but only after paying the five hundred dollar towing fee."

The threat worked, and the driver handed him the requested documents.

"Where are you going?" Bence asked before he looked at what he was handed.

"The Charles de Gaulle Airport."

Bence inspected the documents, focusing on the bill of lading, which listed the shipper, receiver, what was transported, the quantity of goods, their value, and the truck's destination. The bill of lading in his hands had none of these. Instead, it contained two words. "Open the back," Bence demanded.

The driver took a pair of cutters from within the cab, cut the metallic cable security seal, unlocked the cargo doors with a key he removed from his pocket, and opened the two eight feet high doors. Inside were two shipping containers.

"I need to take a closer look," Bence said.

With the driver going first, they climbed the ladder to the cargo bed. Looking at the forty feet long climate-controlled maritime containers, Bence saw that each had stenciled in bold black lettering—in English, French, and another language, the words *Diplomatic Shipment*, precisely what was written on the bill of lading. Below that statement, a plastic-encased paper stated in three languages that Article 27 of the 1961 Vienna Convention on Diplomatic Relations gave the contents of the container diplomatic immunity from search, seizure, or detention. Familiar with customs procedures and protocols, Bence knew this was a diplomatic pouch, the moniker applying to an envelope, bag, or other container used by a diplomatic mission without size or weight limitations.

He looked at the plastic seal affixed to a lock on one of the containers. He saw above it a letter on which a nation's sovereign stamp was embossed onto the paper and the signature of the official authorizing the diplomatic shipment. The letter, containing the delivery address, was encased in plastic and secured with tamper-resistant tape. The second container had the same address. Bence took photos, after which he told the driver to wait beside the truck while he conferred with the officers in the vehicle behind his cruiser. The driver folded his arms and waited.

"Both containers have diplomatic immunity," he said, showing the photos on his phone.

"Are the seals and the letters forgeries?" Donati, who followed Bence to the minivan, asked.

"I've been trained to recognize forgeries and have seen enough seals and letters to know these are authentic. As you can see, the truck is going to the Charles de Gaulle Airport."

"The Mona Lisa may be on that truck," Donais said.

"Or on an earlier one, because I don't think all of Vogel's paintings could fit in two containers."

Everyone was silent, trying to think of what to do next.

"Let's assume this shipment is the last," Bruno said. "Once it gets to the airport, we'll never see the Mona Lisa or the Vatican paintings again."

"What else can we do?" Milani asked. "It's a crime to open a diplomatic pouch."

Hunkler laughed. "We've racked up quite a few crimes in several countries, including planting several individuals in the ground, although they deserved it."

Bence's eyes widened, understanding what Hunkler meant by planting.

"You're right," Milani admitted. "Therefore, I would suggest carpe diem."

"Seize the day?" Donais questioned.

"Take advantage of the unique situation offered us to get not only our paintings but also return those stolen by the Nazis."

"I can go along with that," Hunkler stated.

After the others said they were also committed to returning every stolen painting, everyone looked at Bence.

"I'm in so much trouble now, I hardly think that cutting the locks and seals on diplomatic containers will make much difference," he said.

Bruno decided that searching the containers along the side of the busy expressway would invite photos and postings on social media. Therefore, with Donati in the truck's cab with the driver, the squad car and minivan followed it to the next exit and found a secluded area off the road where they could inspect the containers without being seen.

Because there were thousands of works of art, and sunset was an hour and a half away, they decided to photograph a sampling. After an hour and ten minutes of taking pictures, Bruno decided it was too close to dark to continue. He looked at a map on his cellphone and saw it was around forty-five minutes to the Marseille airport and, with Milani watching, accessed an airline app.

Seeing the destination, the curmudgeon asked if he thought this was where they'd find the Mona Lisa.

"I do," Bruno answered. "Everything is beginning to make sense."

"What do you want to do with the truck and containers?" Hunkler, who was standing near them, asked.

"Can you give this truck a maintenance issue?" Bruno asked, knowing that he had a good understanding of vehicle mechanics.

"How long do you want it out of commission?"

"A minimum of three hours."

"I'll disconnect the brake fluid line. It'll take that long to get a maintenance vehicle here to check out the vehicle, fix the problem, and refill the brake reservoir."

Bruno told him to get started. Once Hunkler left, he went to Bence and asked if he could lean on the driver to say that the delay in getting to Paris was because of a brake fluid leak.

"I can do that," Bence said, walking to where the driver was watching Hunker.

"If I drive this truck, I'll lose my brakes," the driver said, seeing what Hunkler was doing.

"That's not my problem. Call for maintenance, but only after we leave," the colonel responded.

Bence, who stood beside Hunkler, was more diplomatic and gave the driver the context of the situation. "Let me explain a few things," he began. "The paintings in this truck are stolen, and the diplomatic warnings and seals placed on the containers are meant to hide the thefts by keeping anyone from looking inside."

"They're not diplomatic containers?"

"Did you pick them up from an embassy or consulate?" Bence asked.

"No."

"A prosecutor is going to argue it's common sense that, if you picked up containers with diplomatic markings from a private residence, you knew you were carrying something illegal with forged documentation meant to shield it from inspection."

"I'm just a truck driver," he stated, his anxiety elevating the pitch of his voice.

"Ignorance isn't a good defense. As a law enforcement officer, I can say with absolute certainty that you'll be charged with transporting stolen art and being an accessory after the fact to the thefts."

"How could I know what was inside the sealed containers?"

"The prosecutor won't believe you. As I said, ignorance isn't a good defense. You're the low-hanging fruit who's easy to prosecute and to get a guilty verdict from a jury," Bence said.

"I'm innocent," the driver protested.

"Innocent people go to jail all the time. But if you cooperate, I can keep you out of this."

"Anything."

"Does this truck have a GPS tracking device?" Bence asked.

The driver said it did, and that he'd received several calls but hadn't answered them.

"You'll tell whoever's been calling the truck's brake fluid warning light illuminated and, after pulling to the side of the road, you saw the leak and decided to get off the expressway. Is this your rig?" Bence asked.

"No. I'm a contract driver."

"Are you married?" Bruno asked.

"No."

"After you arrive at the airport and park your vehicle, get away from the truck as quickly as possible. When the people who stole these paintings see the containers have been opened, they'll want to speak with you. You won't like how they ask their questions or what I suspect they'll do to you after," Bruno said. "Don't answer your phone for a while and forget everything and everyone you saw."

Bence, who'd written the driver's name and address in his notepad, asked for his cellphone number. Once he received it, he returned his operator's license. "It's time you return that call," he told him.

The caller was Becker, and while Bence was listening, the driver explained the situation with the brake fluid and emphasized the cargo was safe.

"I have your location," Becker said. "I'll get a mobile truck repair service to you."

At 10:30 pm, three hours following his conversation with Vogel's son, the driver was on his way to the Charles de Gaulle Airport. By then, Bruno and his team, accompanied by Bence, were on a plane to where Bruno believed the Mona Lisa was hidden.

"When are they scheduled to land?" Lamberti asked Acardi. He told her.

"Do you think Bruno is right? The French will be coming for their painting tomorrow."

"I don't know," Acardi admitted. "But his explanation makes sense."

"If he's wrong, no amount of damage control will make a difference. Searching diplomatic containers is indefensible. The president will demand Bruno's head to preserve the nation's relationship with an important ally because, if he doesn't, he'll pay a heavy political price. If that's not enough, he may have to put all five behind bars."

"That's unacceptable. We didn't send choirboys after the Mona Lisa. We sent gunslingers whose methods of getting results are decidedly illegal at times."

"This will all play out in the next couple of days. Until then, the only thing we can do is wait and hope our gunslingers tell us they've recovered the paintings," Lamberti said.

"What about Bruno's request?" Acardi asked.

"I think we need to take it up a notch," she replied.

Acardi looked at his watch and believed she was the only one expecting a government official to be awake and working at midnight.

17

Sheik Faisal Al Qasimi became chairperson of the Louvre Abu Dhabi after the disappearance and presumed death of Sheik Walid Al Nahyan. Although each was the head of one of the six ruling families of the United Arab Emirates, there was little commonality between them. Al Nahyan was elected chairperson because he was the leader of Abu Dhabi's ruling family, and not having him serve in that position would have been an insult. The paradox was that Al Nahyan had no interest in art beyond his board responsibilities, preferring to invest in the stock market and companies demonstrating the potential for extraordinary growth. In contrast, Al Qasimi, who resided in Dubai, ninety-three miles north of Abu Dhabi, actively sought to be placed on the board because he loved art and was a knowledgeable and avid collector. It was 9:30 am when, thirty minutes into his board meeting, one of the two cellphones in front of him vibrated. Picking it up, he saw a text from Friedrich Becker that said it was urgent they speak. The sheik recessed the meeting and phoned him from an adjoining room.

"There was a problem with the last two containers," Becker began. "The truck carrying them had a malfunction and was delayed getting to the airport by several hours. However, they arrived in time for their Emirates cargo flight, which will land in Dubai at 4:30 pm."

"I don't see the urgency for this call."

"The airline's warehouse manager told me that the metal seal securing the truck's cargo doors, and the locks and seals on the containers, were missing. I fastened each before they left my residence. Either the driver or someone he knew looked inside."

"Is anything missing?"

"That's unknown since you and I are the only ones with an inventory. Many of the environmental enclosures and boxes were opened, but they didn't take the art. That indicates they were looking for something specific. The manager said, because the containers were very tightly packed, it's doubtful that anything is missing."

"The truck driver will have the answers. Find him, question him, and then put a bullet in his head," Al Qasimi said. "If you have difficulty locating him, let me know. I have a search firm that's very good at finding people."

"Understood. When can I expect the other half of my money?"

"Once I've received all the paintings and verified their authenticity—exactly as we agreed. I have another call," the sheik said, seeing *No Caller ID* appear on his screen and knowing this was common for the select few with his phone number. "We'll speak later."

Thirty minutes after his flight left Marseille, Bruno texted Lamberti and requested the private phone number for Sheik Faisal Al Qasimi. When he landed in Dubai, he'd call the sheik and demand a meeting, during which he'd convince him to return the Mona Lisa and the Vatican paintings. Bruno understood accomplishing that would be a dicey proposition because he couldn't confirm they were in the sheik's possession; he only suspected they were. However, he was out of options, and Al Qasimi was his clear choice for having them.

The Emirates flight from Marseille landed in Dubai on time at a little past seven Saturday morning, two and a half hours before Becker's call with Al Qasimi. Forty-five minutes later—Bruno, Donati, Donais, and Milani were uneasy as they presented their passports, hoping that the now-rescinded red notice for their detention, which originated in the UAE, had been pulled. They cleared customs and immigration without incident.

Because Bruno didn't want to call the sheik for another hour or so, they decided to go for breakfast. Bence suggested the Burj Al Arab because he'd always wanted to see the iconic, sail-shaped hotel. They arrived twenty-five minutes later at 8:30 am.

They went to Sahn Eddar, the atrium restaurant on the first floor. Bruno asked for a table where they could privately discuss their business. The hostess seating them took the hint and brought them to the back of the restaurant, the nearest person four tables away. It was 9:45 am when they finished breakfast, and Bruno called Al Qasimi.

The sheik didn't know the person who, in broken English, was requesting they meet. Therefore, he ended the call without comment, believing it an imprudent solicitation by someone who wanted to enrich themselves with his money. That perception changed a minute later when Bruno sent photos of the stolen art within the containers. Al Qasimi answered his next call on the first ring.

"I'm listening," the sheik said, his voice imbued with self-importance.

"My associates and I want a face-to-face meeting."

"Not without knowing what this is about."

"You already know. You're the recipient of stolen paintings sent by Reinhard Vogel's son and attorney, Friedrich Becker. They were transported in containers from his home to the Charles de Gaulle Airport and flown here. Each container had diplomatic markings so that customs wouldn't open it. Am I being specific enough, or should I continue to waste our time?" Bruno asked.

"Where are you?"

"In the Sahn Eddar restaurant at the Burj Al Arab."

"I'm in Abu Dhabi. I'll be in my Dubai office by noon. We'll meet there at that time."

"I prefer a public venue. Let's meet here at noon," Bruno said, ending the call without giving Al Qasimi time to respond.

The sheik entered the restaurant at precisely noon with six bodyguards in tow. His entourage sat at the three empty tables beside Bruno and his group, effectively preventing anyone from getting close enough to hear what was said. The sheik, who wore a long white robe and white headscarf, was five feet nine inches tall, thin, and had a closely cropped black beard that displayed three days of growth.

The six stood when Al Qasimi approached, and no handshakes were exchanged when Bruno introduced himself and the others. During this time, the guards sent away the servers approaching the table with menus and bottled water.

"I'm listening," the sheik said as he sat in the empty chair to the left of Bruno, who told him in detail about Al Nahyan's involvement in the theft of art and the association with Reinhard Vogel, who possessed an extensive collection of art that was looted by the Nazis. "The stolen and looted paintings were inside the containers sent to you."

"Since you haven't any proof beyond the photos, and my government has no documentation on the contents of these diplomatic containers, I'd say all you have is a story orchestrated to embarrass me."

"Orchestrated?" Bence said, interrupting Bruno's response. "Look at these," he said, showing Al Qasimi photos of the paperwork designating him as the consignee for the diplomatic containers.

"Forgeries."

"No one is going to believe your claim of innocence once they see the extent of our evidence."

"I'll claim everything is forged," the sheik arrogantly responded.

"That will be difficult to substantiate. We have photos of a document affixed to each container, signed by an official from your government. These diplomatic letters have your nation's sovereign stamp embossed on them and designate you as the consignee. While you might erase all evidence of this shipment arriving in Dubai, they'll be a customs record at Charles de Gaulle Airport for them leaving the country uninspected. For that to occur, customs would have validated the authenticity of the documentation on each container, designating it a diplomatic pouch. Additionally, we have numerous photos of the stolen paintings within them. I have more than enough evidence to prove you're the recipient and orchestrator of art stolen from several nations."

"And your solution for me not to be muddied by these accusations?"

"I want the immediate return of the Mona Lisa and the two Vatican paintings," Bruno replied, not recalling the names of those paintings.

"Da Vinci's Saint Jerome in the Wilderness and Raphael's Transfiguration," Milani quickly clarified.

"I also want every stolen work of art returned. Make up any story you like. You can tell the world how, under your direction, the UAE broke an international smuggling ring. Make up your own story; I don't care," Bruno said.

"And in return for my half a billion dollar payment for the paintings and relinquishing control of all but the stolen art, what compromise do you propose?" the sheik asked.

"You keep the non-stolen works; you don't have the stigma of being a dealer in stolen art; and you enhance your stature in the world's art community by confiscating and returning the stolen paintings."

"That compromise falls pitifully short of equivalence. My stature doesn't require enhancement because I'm the chair of a major museum and the leader of one of the six ruling families in my country. Let me be clear. I have the money and status to spin these accusations to make everyone at this table look like you were trying to extort money from me. A pitiful group of investigators and an elderly curator trying to fleece a wealthy art patron will be a believable story."

"You took an immense risk. Why?" Bruno asked.

"I have an extraordinary love of art and went to considerable expense so that I can enjoy the magnificence and beauty of these masterpieces within my palace in solitude," the sheik said, pointing out the window to what looked to be a small hotel across the water.

"Your palace?" Bruno asked.

The sheik nodded and smiled for the first time as Bruno continued to look at the massive structure. "You might be able to raid the home of an aging man living out his last weeks as cancer consumes him, but not the head of an Emirati royal family."

"Reinhard Vogel is dying?" Donati asked, wondering if he'd heard correctly.

"He has between two weeks and a month to live. How do you think I was able to buy his collection? His son isn't an aesthete like his father. The only art he appreciates are the engravings on Euro currencies."

"How did you meet Reinhard Vogel?" Donati continued.

"When Sheik Walid Al Nahyan discovered Vogel was dying, he introduced him."

"Why?"

"He knew I'd be interested in purchasing his paintings because, like him, my collection is not for the enjoyment of

184 | ALAN REFKIN

others. Introducing me was also his way of ensuring Vogel's son didn't try fencing the art, which might expose him."

"From what I heard, Sheik Al Nahyan was wealthy enough to purchase the art without your involvement," Bruno interjected.

"And then what, keep them in containers forever? He was a pragmatist and knew I'd jump at the chance to obtain the unobtainable."

"And Vogel liked that his art collection would be intact and live on, so to speak," Donais stated, drawing a hard stare from Al Qasimi because, in his country, women never interjected in a discussion between men.

"The father had little choice," Al Qasimi responded, ignoring Donais and looking at Bruno. "I offered to pay fair market value for his legitimate paintings, which he could sell at auction because their provenance was intact, and a percentage of the estimated value of the stolen works. Money was wired to an offshore account."

"Except neither the father nor the son was as careful as you expected, leaving a trail that led to Sheik Walid Al Nahyan and you," Bruno said.

"It was careless to put me as the consignee. I'd given the son the name and address of a fictitious company and told him to put that on the customs documents and bills of ladings. That he didn't do it was astonishingly inept."

"Did you ask him why?"

"He said he wanted to make sure that I received the containers. Otherwise, they might get lost with a fictitious name and address, as if they could with customs in my city expecting their arrival and having instructions to deliver them uninspected to my home."

"That mistake brought us here," Bruno stated.

"I assume you killed the sheik," Al Qasimi said, changing the subject, "and that a continued search for him and the others is pointless?"

"That's a valid assumption. Were you related?"

"Distantly. The UAE is a federation of six emirates that came together in 1971, the seventh joining the following year. There are six ruling families. Although each royal family has a different origin, those of Abu Dhabi and Dubai descend from the same tribe, making us distantly related," the sheik said, rising to his feet. "With nothing further to discuss, this meeting is over."

"One last question," Bruno said as he stood. "Since this is likely the last time we'll see or speak to one another, you haven't told me if you have the Mona Lisa and the Vatican's paintings."

"I'll let you figure that out," the sheik said before leaving the room.

"What do you think?" Milani asked once he'd left.

"That we're screwed."

Bruno called Acardi, who conferenced Lamberti into the call. He began by summarizing his conversation with the sheik.

"I'm surprised he came to the meeting," Acardi said.

"He wanted to pick my brain. In the end, he found out what we knew and believed he had the power and money to spin this so that we'll be the villains, not to mention that he's untouchable in the UAE. What's disappointing is that we don't know if he has the paintings or if we've gone down the wrong rabbit hole."

"I hate to be the bearer of more bad news, but the Vatican received word that the Louvre intends to pick up the Mona Lisa at 12:01 am tomorrow," Acardi said.

"That's twelve hours ahead of schedule. Why so early?" Bruno asked.

"Because they want to put it back on display at the Louvre that day. They've already announced its return, and even though it's the middle of the night, the media will follow the Mona Lisa from the moment the chartered aircraft lands in Paris until its arrival by motorcade."

"I'm told the last two containers arrive in Dubai at 4:30 pm," Lamberti said.

"Why is that important?" Bruno questioned.

"It's a matter of timing. I want you there when the plane lands. I took a hands-on approach and expanded on what you asked me to do earlier."

"Would you care to explain?"

Lamberti did.

"That was brilliant. Will the sheik go along?"

"I don't believe he'll be given a choice."

18

The Emirates cargo flight from Paris arrived at five-thirty, an hour later than expected. A large storm, lingering between Europe and the Middle East, necessitated that air traffic control divert aircraft around it, creating narrow corridors into which the planes were sequenced and substantially extending flight times.

Once the Boeing 777F landed, the tower directed the pilot to taxi to the Al Majlis VIP Terminal, a first for him because cargo aircraft didn't transport VIPs, and he didn't believe they wanted to offload the giant freighter's cargo there. Nevertheless, he followed the tower's instructions, confused at the reason for the change. His confusion elevated thirty seconds later when the VIP terminal came into view, and he saw a podium surrounded by a standing crowd of approximately thirty. Sitting in chairs behind the podium were thirteen people, six wearing a kandura with a headscarf held in place with an agal, and seven dressed in western-style business attire. That one of them was a woman made the grouping all the more surreal.

The pilot shut down his right engine to reduce the noise and the hurricane-like air coming from it and, following the ground crew's hand signals, stopped the plane with its right wing tip one hundred feet from the podium. He then turned off his left engine and switched on the aircraft's auxiliary power unit, a small jet engine located in the tail. The power generated by it provided electricity to the aircraft's systems, including the cargo door, without relying on a ground power unit, which was inherently noisy. As the pilot was switching to internal power, two large forklifts were brought into position outside the pilot-side cargo door. When the hatch opened and the dark blue containers came into view, they were quickly removed and placed side-by-side on the ground.

The president of the United Arab Emirates, Sheik Tariq Al Besher, stepped to the podium, tapped the microphone to ensure it worked, and began his prepared speech. Behind him were four cabinet-level ministers, including the Minister of Finance, and Sheik Faisal Al Qasimi, whose normally placid demeanor was replaced by an expression of contempt at what was occurring. To the left of the sheik were Mauro Bruno and his team members, who were there at the invitation of the president, and the Italian ambassador to the UAE. Approximately thirty members of the media and their film crews were also present, fifteen on either side of the attendees.

Originally, Bruno asked Lamberti to convince the Minister of Finance to pressure Al Qasimi into returning the stolen paintings. She took it a step further by calling the president of the UAE, who conferenced the minister into their conversation. After listening to Lamberti, Al Besher directed him to orchestrate what was unfolding beside the aircraft.

As museum staff began removing and carefully opening some of the boxes within the containers, Al Besher explained that the UAE's Signal Intelligence Agency, the counterpart to America's National Security Agency, in cooperation with the Italian government, broke an international smuggling ring that stole some of the world's most valuable art and replaced it with near-perfect forgeries. He went on to say that the large transport containers in front of them were only two of the many recovered, some of which were found to have paintings looted by the Nazis and thought to be lost forever. The president promised that a list of the recovered art would be made available and that the paintings would be under heavy security at the Shindagha Museum until returned to their rightful owners.

Because this was the UAE and not the United States or a European country, the press didn't interrupt the president nor shout questions, one of which might have been why an international smuggling operation capable of such thefts had retained such an extensive inventory of art and not sold it. Otherwise, what was the point of a theft that cost the thief money since, in many cases, they replaced the originals with forgeries? The follow-up questions might have been what led them to the location of the art, how it was recovered without apprehending a single person, and why weren't the names of those involved in the thefts given.

Following the president's speech, the four stolen paintings the museum staff had removed from their boxes were positioned on either side of the president so that he would be at the center of every photo sent to global media outlets. Once the press left, Al Besher invited his guests inside the VIP terminal. At the same time, the museum staff re-boxed the paintings, and security loaded the containers onto a large flatbed truck for transport to the museum.

"I need a private word with you," the sheik said to the president when they entered the terminal.

Al Besher asked those around him to partake of the refreshments at the back of the room, implying that he wanted to be alone with Al Qasimi.

"If you hadn't opened those containers and shown the art, there wouldn't be a shred of proof these paintings were in our country. You let the foreigners win," Al Qasimi said, the disgust evident in his voice.

"Do you believe the most famous museums in the world would ever stop looking for their art and that, even after your death, your thievery would remain undiscovered? Our families are worth hundreds of billions—our wealth derived from oil, tourism, and investments. What would happen if, because of your actions, the world's trust in our integrity evaporates and turns to mistrust and disdain?"

"We don't need foreigners; they need us."

"We're a global society that became rich by selling oil, tourism, and commodities and investing the profits from these enterprises. Your fixation on paintings, irrational acquisition of stolen art, and selfishness might have been catastrophic had not the Italians intervened. I meant what I said. Every stolen painting will be returned. Tomorrow, you'll resign from the board of the Louvre Abu Dhabi and devote your efforts to something other than art."

"I can't do that. It's my lifelong passion."

"But you will because I've so decreed, and noncompliance comes with financial consequences to your family," the president said in a stern voice that Al Qasimi had rarely heard from the mild-mannered monarch.

The president, whose cellphone was chiming nonstop during his conversation, removed it from his pocket, seeing a multitude of texts from world leaders applauding what he'd done. After dismissing Al Qasimi with a wave of his hand, he found the Italian ambassador at the back of the room and asked him to thank Pia Lamberti for her suggestions and discretion. As they conversed, Bruno looked at his watch and approached them.

"Thank you for intervening and returning the art in those containers to the world," Bruno said.

"It was the right thing to do," the president responded.

"I wish we could have confirmed if Sheik Al Qasimi had the Mona Lisa and Vatican paintings."

"He doesn't have them," Al Besher said. "I sent the museum staff and my security guards to search his palace, where they discovered and took possession of the other containers of stolen art. The Mona Lisa wasn't among the art they seized."

"In seven and a half hours, the Louvre Paris will be at the Vatican for a masterpiece we don't have. The French will go ballistic," Bruno said.

"Ms. Lamberti shared the difficulties you encountered in retrieving these paintings. You thanked me for intervening and returning the stolen art to the world. However, I should thank you because my country took credit for your remarkable actions. To express my appreciation, I'd like to offer my aircraft for your return to Rome," the president said, pointing to the Boeing 747-400VIP aircraft in the distance. "It's fueled and ready to depart for the Ciampino Airport, which I'm told is twenty miles from the Vatican. Also, in appreciation, there are three parting gifts onboard the aircraft," Al Besher said.

"Are they what I think they are?"

"Yes," Al Besher confirmed.

"But you said that Sheik Al Qasimi didn't have them."

"He didn't. They were hanging in Sheik Al Nahyan's office."

"I was told he didn't care about art."

"I believe he stole and kept the paintings to torment Sheik Al Qasimi."

"Why didn't Al Qasimi steal it when the sheik went missing?"

"He didn't have an opportunity. After his disappearance, I sent my security team to Al Nahyan's residence to speak with his staff to see if they knew where he might have gone after leaving the shipping company. When one went to his office to look for a calendar or something that would explain his whereabouts, he saw the paintings. I went to his residence believing they were reproductions because the sheik wasn't an art collector, but I had to be sure. When asked, his staff said they were authentic and confessed what the sheik had done."

"They could have lied."

"In my country, lying to the sovereign would cost them their life that day. Enough talk. You need to leave. I'm told the flight to Rome is six hours and fifteen minutes, meaning you'll land around 11:15 pm."

The pilot, having been told by the president to get everyone to Rome as quickly as possible, didn't waste any time. He started the four engines before the six boarded and, with other aircraft told to hold in place, taxied onto runway 30 right and accelerated down the fourteen thousand feet strip of concrete. Once airborne, Milani opened the boxes and examined each painting.

"Are they authentic?" Bruno asked after the curmudgeon finished examining the last painting. When Milani said they were, he called Acardi and Lamberti.

"If you drive, it'll take thirty minutes to get from Ciampino to the Vatican," Lamberti said. "I'll ask the pope to send his helicopter. You'll be here in less than ten minutes."

"Have the Mona Lisa's environmental enclosure in the helicopter. I'll have Milani put the painting into it on the way to save time because whoever's coming from the Louvre will expect it to be in the same enclosure in which they sent the fake to us," Bruno said. As he was about to end his call, the copilot approached and told him that the same weather that affected the Emirates freighter was now impacting them. He repeated what was said to Lamberti and put his phone on speaker.

"Going through one of the bypass corridors will extend our flying time by about thirty minutes, even with our VIP designation," the copilot continued.

"What would that make our estimated time of arrival?"

"11:45 pm."

"That puts us in Vatican City with five minutes to spare if everything goes perfectly," Bruno said.

After the copilot returned to the cockpit, Bruno asked Lamberti if she'd heard their new ETA.

"We'll deal with it. Acardi and I will be waiting at the Vatican. Keep me up to date," she said before ending the call.

At 11:30 pm, the pope received a call that the Louvre's curator and his staff had arrived.

"They're thirty minutes early," Lamberti said.

"They're at the Via Della Conciliazione entrance near Saint Peter's Basilica," the pope replied. "We should be thankful they didn't come to the Vatican's lesser-known Viale Vaticano entrance, which is virtually across from us."

Acardi unconsciously looked in that direction since he and Lamberti were familiar with the Vatican's layout and had come through it. They, the pope, and the Swiss Guards were the only ones in the Room of the Creed. The Vatican Museums' curator had been with them but was sent home by the pontiff because he was an emotional wreck. With the original Mona Lisa still not at the Vatican, no amount of Xanax could get rid of the anxiety he was displaying.

Because the Vatican didn't own a helicopter, the Italian Air Force provided one on request. If the pope said he needed it, they dispatched an Agusta Westland to the Vatican's helipad. That request was always made by a member of the pontiff's staff. However, when the pope called instead, the officer on duty sensed the urgency of the situation and dispatched the Agusta Westland that was on base alert rather than waiting for a crew to drive from their homes to a helicopter that needed to be prepped for flight.

The Agusta Westland set down on the helipad shortly after it was summoned. With its rotors still turning, Acardi put the environmental display case into the passenger area and then donned one of the aircraft's headsets.

"The pope isn't coming?" the pilot asked.

"Time is short. I can't tell you why, but it's critical you get to Ciampino and bring the people and what they're carrying here as fast as possible."

The aircraft commander was a fifteen-year veteran and had orders from an officer several ranks above him to do whatever the Vatican wanted until he was released to return to base. Therefore, he didn't need to know why something needed to happen, only that it did. Once the aircraft was on its way to Ciampino, Acardi returned to the Apostolic Palace.

"We need to stall the team from the Louvre," Lamberti said to the pontiff as Acardi entered the room.

"I know," he replied.

With impeccable timing, the Swiss Guard told him of the curator's arrival.

"Tell them the Vatican will take possession of its paintings first and escort them to my apartment at the Domus Sanctae Marthae. I'm not permitting vehicles or electric carts within Vatican City until morning. They'll need to carry the paintings there."

The guard left without comment.

"Your apartment is a solid fifteen-minute walk from here," Acardi said. "Won't they find it suspicious delivering the paintings to a residential building?"

"Not when I tell them the truth—that there's no staff working at this hour and that my apartment is under constant watch by the Swiss Guard. Once I sign for the paintings, the Louvre's responsibility for their security ends, and I don't believe they'll care where I keep them after that. But this delay may not be long enough. We need to do something else to buy us time."

"What?" Acardi asked.

"I wish I knew," the pope answered.

"The storm has expanded, and there's now only one corridor around it. We'll be in a holding pattern until it's our turn to transit. That makes twelve-fifteen our new ETA," the pilot said to Bruno. "However, if the storm expands, the corridor will get narrower, meaning fewer planes can simultaneously pass through it, and we'll be delayed further."

"Can you see this bad boy on your instruments?" Bruno asked.

He pointed to the weather radar. "As a rule, the brighter the color, the more severe the weather. Light and dark blue are areas of low precipitation; yellow denotes moderate rain; orange means heavy rain; red indicates heavy precipitation; and purple tells the pilot the rain will be extremely heavy and possibly contain hail."

"How does this aircraft fly in moderate rain?"

"It'll get bumpy—not much different from driving on a Detroit street. I know what you're thinking, but there's a red cell on either side of the yellow area in front of us. If they expand, we'll be inside a red cell. That's why there are no aircraft going through the yellow area. It's too dangerous."

"Let's assume the yellow and red areas remain stable. How long would it take to get past the storm?" Bruno asked.

"Depending on the turbulence within the cell, fifteen minutes, plus or minus."

"It's critical I get to the Vatican. Seconds count," Bruno pleaded.

The former UAE military pilot knew his passengers had to be extremely important to warrant the exclusive use of the president's aircraft. "Alright, we'll give it a go," the pilot said. "Tell the cabin attendant to make sure all loose items are secured, and that everyone is buckled tightly into their seats because this may be a rough ride."

Once Bruno left the cockpit, the pilot informed air traffic control that he'd like a vector through the moderate section of the storm. The ATC controller immediately asked him to repeat what he'd said, believing he misunderstood the request because he'd never known a pilot who wanted to enter a storm.

"I want a vector through the yellow area on your weather screen," the pilot clarified.

"I strongly advise against it," the controller unambiguously stated. "There's a red cell on either side of it."

"I'm aware of the risks, but my flight is time sensitive."

Knowing this was a presidential aircraft and not wanting to cause an incident, the controller reluctantly granted the request and gave the pilot a vector through the center of the yellow area on his weather radar, adding for the benefit of the tower's recording that entering the storm was at the pilot's request. Cleared to proceed, the pilot tightened his harness, banked the aircraft fifteen degrees to the right to intercept the vector he was given, and retarded the throttles on the Boeing 747-400 to maneuvering speed where the aircraft would stall before reaching its load limit, thereby protecting the plane from damage in severe turbulence.

As it entered the yellow cell, the aircraft began to mildly buffet, vibrating in the wind and rain that pelted the aircraft. Nothing worse happened for the first three minutes, the six passengers believing what they were experiencing was as bad as it would get. However, that sentiment wasn't shared by the flight crew, who saw on their scope that the two red cells were converging around them, and there was no way to avoid what was about to happen.

Pressing the intercom button, the pilot told everyone in a strained voice to keep their seatbelts tight and hold on to anything they could because the aircraft was about to encounter extreme turbulence. A heartbeat later, the half-million-pound plane was abruptly thrown three thousand feet up, followed by a rapid drop of a thousand feet a moment later as the shearing winds played with the aircraft and lightning illuminated the surrounding skies. This rollercoaster effect, punctuated at times by lateral gusts that pivoted the aircraft sideways, kept repeating with the rain so intense that the plane seemed underwater to anyone who could look at the darkened skies during the intermittent flashes of thunder.

The aircraft's violent maneuvers lasted ten minutes but seemed substantially longer to the passengers. Over the next five minutes, the rain gradually subsided, the lightning disappeared, the skies brightened, and the air became as smooth as glass. Bruno unfastened his seatbelt and saw that the others seemed shaken but unhurt, and that the cabin attendant was out of their seat and checking on them. Walking to the cockpit, he poked his head inside.

"That was a wild ride," Bruno told the pilot.

"Is everyone alright?"

"A few barf bags were used. Otherwise, not a scratch, thanks to your flying. I'm guessing the two red cells merged."

"That's precisely what happened. The good news is you're back on schedule, and we should have wheels on the ground around 11:45 this evening."

The pilot beat that estimate and landed at the Ciampino Airport at 11:40 pm. Ground control directed the aircraft to the private terminal parking apron where the fifteen-passenger Agusta Westland AW139 helicopter was waiting. However, the airport catered to discount airlines and private aircraft much smaller than the Boeing 747-400. Therefore, when the giant plane came to a stop, the tower informed the pilot that the airport didn't have a deplaning ramp that was high enough to reach its hatch, but the manager on duty was looking for a solution. The pilot told Bruno.

"This is unbelievable," Bruno said.

"It's a first for me," the pilot admitted.

"I need to get to the Vatican by midnight, no matter what."

"There's a way, but it'll piss off everyone at this terminal because it'll mean this plane will be stuck where it is, blocking the private terminal for the better part of the day."

"I'm desperate," Bruno said.

"Then follow me," the pilot replied. Walking down the stairway to the main deck, he armed the front entry hatch and shoved it open. When he did, it pulled the slide pack out of its bustle and ejected a pin from a squib containing compressed gas. The slide quickly inflated.

Moments later, Bruno went down the slide holding the container with the Mona Lisa. Hunkler and Donati followed, each holding one of the Vatican's paintings. The others were next. Once everyone was onboard the helicopter, the aircrew started the Agusta Westland's two Pratt & Whitney turboshaft engines, lifting off at 11:55 pm.

"If you would sign these, Holiness," the curator said, presenting the one-page transfer papers to the pontiff, one set in Italian and the other in French.

The pope spent as much time as he believed reasonable to read and sign the transfer papers.

"And now, we'd like to return the noblewoman Lisa del Giocondo to France," the curator said, referring to the subject of da Vinci's masterpiece.

"Please follow me," the pope said, leaving the papal apartment with his Swiss Guard escort. It was one-minute past midnight.

"How long until we land?" Bruno asked.

"Two minutes," the pilot answered.

Hunkler used an electric screwdriver from the aircraft toolkit to remove the twenty-four screws securing the Mona Lisa's environmental enclosure; Milani placing the Mona Lisa within its enclosure as the helicopter descended toward the helipad. Once the painting was secure, Hunkler began putting the screws back in place, finishing thirty seconds after the helicopter kissed the landing pad. During the descent, Bruno called Acardi.

"The pope left his apartment with the Louvre's curator and staff a minute ago."

"Any ideas on how we get to the Apostolic Palace ahead of them?" Bruno nervously asked.

"Wait there," Acardi said without explanation as the connection went dead.

Everyone was unhappy at waiting, overcoming what seemed to be insurmountable obstacles and driven during the past two weeks by a rock-solid determination to get the Mona Lisa to the Vatican before the curator arrived.

The Vatican's helipad was a rectangular concrete area at the western edge of the Vatican Gardens, an area of fifty-seven acres comprising half the country. Seeing the road at the edge of the landing pad, Bruno asked the pilots if they had driven to the helipad, hoping their vehicles were nearby. However, the pilot dashed that hope when he said the helicopter belonged to the Italian Air Force and they flew to the Vatican only on request.

"Can you fly me across the Vatican Garden and drop me at the Apostolic Palace?" Bruno asked.

The pilot said they were prohibited from landing anywhere in Vatican City except the helipad because the high-velocity air created by the aircraft could reach one hundred fifteen mph and damage the centuries-old buildings, statues, stained-glass windows, and antiquities that were prevalent.

Bruno knew that restriction made sense. As he looked at his watch and saw that it was eight minutes past midnight, he heard a fast-approaching vehicle and saw it was Lamberti's extended-length Range Rover. Screeching to a stop beside the helipad, Acardi rolled down the passenger window and yelled to put the paintings in the cargo compartment and for everyone to get in. They did, and he took off like a Formula One racer down the Viale Vaticano toward the second Vatican entrance. It was nine minutes past midnight.

The curator and his staff, invigorated by the imminent return of the Mona Lisa, wanted to speed-walk to the Apostolic Palace. The pope, trying to slow the pace, was in snail mode. One hundred yards from his apartment, the curator became frustrated by his slowness. Coming up with a good excuse to not insult the pontiff, he told him that, to save time at this late hour, he was going ahead to validate the Mona Lisa and sign the return documents while his staff accompanied him to the Apostolic Palace.

The pope, finding himself in the impossible position of not wanting the curator to arrive at the Room of the Creed without him and unable to force everyone to continue at a snail's pace, said the exercise would do him good and lengthened his stride. Although the pace wasn't as robust as the curator would have liked, he had no choice but to go along. At twelve minutes past midnight, the Apostolic Palace came into view.

It took Acardi five minutes to get from the helipad to the Viale Vaticano gate, the guard raising the barrier at fourteen minutes past midnight. As they pulled in front of the Apostolic Palace, they saw the pope and the group from the Louvre entering the building.

"What now?" Bruno asked.

Acardi didn't answer, calling Lamberti instead, telling her they were outside with the Mona Lisa but couldn't enter the building without being seen.

"I'll handle it. Bring the Mona Lisa inside now," she said.

"Now?"

"Now," she repeated.

Lamberti greeted the curator and his team and ushered them into an anteroom with the pope, who didn't have a clue what she was up to. She then closed the door behind them. Because she was expensively dressed, had an aristocratic stature, and looked important, the curator wondered what this was about and didn't object.

After she introduced herself as a representative of the president of Italy, the curator believed this would be a time-wasting political speech and wanted to push her aside, take possession of the Mona

Lisa, and return to Paris. However, he was stuck listening to her word salad for several minutes, in which she thanked the French government for allowing da Vinci's masterpiece to be displayed at the Vatican and hoped that Italy would also have an opportunity to exchange meaningful works of art with the Louvre. The curator thanked her on behalf of his government and started for the door, only to stop in his tracks when she asked the pontiff to speak. The pontiff started with a prayer, which held the anxious curator in place. He followed by expressing his thanks to the French government, saying he looked forward to further exchanges between the Vatican and Louvre. It was seventeen minutes past midnight when Lamberti opened the door to the anteroom and led the way into the Room of the Creed.

Seeing the Mona Lisa for the first time in two weeks and oblivious to those around him, the curator took five minutes to inspect the masterpiece. With skills similar to Milani, his confident smile said he had back in his possession the most famous painting in the world.

19

The photo of the Boeing 747-400 with a deployed evacuation slide spread like wildfire across social media platforms and was on the front page of *Corriere della Sera*, Italy's oldest and most-read newspaper. Because the aircraft's tail number gave away its ownership, the president of the UAE needed a plausible story as to what his aircraft was doing in Italy and why it landed at the Ciampino airport. That was given to him by Lamberti, the official Emeriti press release stating the aircraft was on its way to Rome for an unannounced meeting between officials in both governments when an equipment malfunction necessitated the giant aircraft land at the nearest airport, which was Ciampino, the deployment of the landing door being the only way for the passengers and crew to disembark the disabled aircraft. The presence of the Italian army helicopter beside it was explained as a nighttime training exercise, which was canceled to take those onboard the presidential 747 to the UAE embassy. Conspiracy theorists, which in this situation were spot on, brought up that both airports were only nineteen miles apart and, unless a plane was missing a piece or two from its airframe or was plummeting from the sky like a rock, this was a negligible distance given the aircraft was descending from thirty-five thousand feet. However, most people discounted this, preferring the more straightforward explanation that the plane was in trouble and looked for the closest airport.

Edgard Bence arrived in Paris on the French government's Falcon 7X aircraft reserved for senior government officials. Upon landing, he was taken to the Élysée Palace, where the president of France greeted him like a long-lost brother, air-kissing him on the right cheek and then the left. If the president's aide had not called beforehand and explained what transpired in the past thirty-six hours, Bence would have thought he was dreaming in his jail cell at La Santé Prison.

What precipitated Bence's change of circumstances was that the presidents of the United Arab Emirates and Italy had called his country's head of state and touted his invaluable help, saying that thousands of stolen works of art would never have been recovered without it. That many of them were taken from French museums and families during the Second World War substantially elevated what he'd done in the eyes of the president and made him a national hero. Unknown to him, Lamberti had orchestrated both calls.

That afternoon, in front of press and government dignitaries, Captain Edgard Bence was promoted to the rank of major and awarded the Honour Medal of the National Police, the nation's highest honor for a law enforcement officer, which the president deemed to apply to officers working in the Directorate-General of Customs and Indirect Taxes. Bence's new position was to command the Mission for Research and Restitution of Spoliated Cultural Property, charged with searching for artwork looted during World War II.

Milani was appointed Curator of the Vatican Museums for Life after the pope suggested the present curator retire. The curmudgeon's first task was to replace the two fake paintings returned by the French with the original works he'd brought from the UAE. Afterward, he went to lunch at the Bistrot La Pigna, where he received a standing ovation from its patrons, the Vatican having earlier announced his lifetime appointment. Later that day, Dante Acardi brought Pasqual Ortega to the curator's office, fulfilling a promise made by Lamberti that the talented forger would enter a training program to become a restoration specialist, a profession he embraced. "If this experience has taught me anything," Ortega said to Milani, "it's that no matter how good I was, it was only a matter of time until someone like you discovered my imperfections, and I'd be arrested."

"That's smart. Most don't learn that lesson until they're behind bars," Acardi said. "This is from Ms. Lamberti," he continued, handing Ortega an envelope.

"What's this?"

"Open it."

Ortega did, finding a key and a piece of paper with an address written on it.

"The key is to an apartment several blocks from the Vatican. You can walk to work. Now that you've taken a substantial pay cut, the government is paying your rent while in training."

"Does my apartment have a northern light?" Ortega asked, playing with Acardi.

"Not unless you punch a hole through a brick wall," he answered with a smile.

The day after his promotion to major, Bence returned to Saint-Jean-Cap-Ferrat and pressed the intercom button on the post beside the gate to Friedrich Becker's home. The attorney, who'd been expecting him after seeing the media coverage of his award and promotion ceremony at the Élysée Palace, and the president of the UAE announcing his country's recovery of stolen art, opened the gate and waited by the front door for him to arrive.

"Have you come to search for terrorists?" Becker asked, making the snide remark to Bence and the two officers accompanying him.

"I'm here to arrest you."

"On what charge?"

"Charges," Bence clarified, handing him the arrest warrant.

"Are you also going to arrest my father?" Becker asked.

"I was told he has between two weeks and a month to live."

"It's closer to a week."

"He can spend his last days in peace. The almighty can judge him."

"These charges are imaginative," Becker stated, glancing at the dozen crimes listed. "But you haven't any evidence linking me to the stolen art from which all of these charges stem."

"The Emirati government has given me the serial numbers of the forty feet long climate-controlled containers in which the stolen art was transported to their country. They were purchased at the Port of Marseille with your credit card."

"I lost a credit card on a business trip to Marseille."

"That's convenient. If I understand correctly, the thief who stole your credit card and purchased the containers filled them with stolen art, found your address and, for an inexplicable reason, brought them to your residence before taking them to Charles de Gaulle Airport. I expected more creativity from an attorney."

"Creativity is unnecessary because these charges will never be heard in a court of law. For an officer, you're quite ignorant. Have you heard of the fruit of the forbidden tree? It means that illegally obtained evidence is inadmissible in court. From the moment you entered my father's home on the pretext that he was involved in terrorist activities, everything that followed was inadmissible. That argument extends to me. When I get done with you, you'll go from national hero to national disgrace in less than a day."

"I agree with everything you've said, counselor. That's why I've decided to take a different approach and streamline the judicial process."

"What does that mean?"

"That I'm not enforcing the warrant. I only filed it to justify your disappearance."

"I'm not running. Why would I? I can't be convicted of these charges," Becker said, throwing the warrant at Bence.

"I know, although you and your father should be behind bars for these crimes and murder, although I can't prove it."

"We didn't murder anyone."

"But you hired those who did. You orchestrated the hit-and-run traffic accident that killed the Louvre's restoration specialist, who substituted the fake Mona Lisa for the original. In case you forgot, his name was Preuet Dages. How many other restoration specialists met a similar fate?"

"They knew too much," Becker admitted. "Again, you have no proof, only conjecture. The police have ruled each an accident. Case closed."

"As you said, I can't prove it, and the judicial system will never convict you of the crimes listed in the warrant. That's why I'm taking another approach. You're going to disappear. These officers, who view you as slime under their shoes, are taking you to an Emirati diplomatic aircraft going to Abu Dhabi, where a court has convicted you in absentia of selling stolen art to the royal family and sentenced you to prison."

"You're bluffing. This is your way of negotiating a deal between us. Okay, let's hear your offer."

Bence ignored the remark. "You were given a speedy trial thanks to the Emirati president's intervention, found guilty, and sentenced to thirty years in prison. Because it was your first offense, the president has graciously commuted it to twenty-five years."

"You're kidnapping a French citizen. I'll make my voice heard from prison, where I'll become an international celebrity while you're rotting in a cell for the rest of your life."

"You don't understand your situation. You're going to a black prison where you'll never speak to an attorney, a French embassy official, the press, or anyone beyond your incarceration center. No one in France will know where you are. They'll believe you're hiding, in France or elsewhere, because of the seriousness of the accusations made against you in the warrant."

"I'll find a way to get out."

"Let me give you some advice."

"What's that?"

"Don't be yourself, which means an arrogant prick. This prison is in the deep desert, and I'm told that problem prisoners become irretrievably lost when on work patrol."

Becker didn't have a response and, with those words, Bence nodded to the officers who cuffed their screaming prisoner, put duct tape over his mouth, and threw him into the police van.

Bruno, Donati, and Donais left for Milan the same morning the Mona Lisa returned to the Louvre. They spent the following week getting much-needed rest and going through the stack of mail that accumulated in their absence. They were at their communal desk, which also served as their conference table, when they heard a knock on the door. Bruno opened it and saw the intruder was Acardi.

"Come in, Dante," he said as Donati and Donais took notice of their visitor and joined him.

"I've come to deliver this," he said, removing a check from his inside jacket pocket and handing it to Bruno.

"That's very generous," he said after looking at the amount. Bruno handed the check to Donais, with Donati looking over her shoulder.

"This is far beyond what we would have invoiced," Donais said.

"Call the difference a bonus for extraordinary performance and hazardous duty."

Bruno and Donati, who once worked for Acardi, knew he wasn't known for his generosity, nor for coming to see someone for strictly social reasons. There was a reason he flew to see them rather than wire the money to their corporate account, which he had on file. Therefore, Acardi's two former employees waited for the other shoe to drop, which it did thirty minutes later when Bruno brought him a second cup of espresso.

"The president, Ms. Lamberti, and I continue to be impressed with your intuitiveness and performance," Acardi began.

"Colonel Hunkler and Dottore Milani were critical to our success. It's no exaggeration to say we'd be dead without the colonel's intervention and would have never found the Mona Lisa without the doctor's expertise," Bruno stated.

"That's why for your next assignment, the pope has offered to let Colonel Hunkler accompany you," Acardi said, looking like he'd just announced they had the winning lottery ticket.

Bruno, who was used to his craftiness, asked if that meant the assignment was dangerous because, he stated, Hunkler's primary skill was causing trauma to anyone standing in the way.

"Would I knowingly send you into a situation where the odds were heavily against your survival?"

"Without hesitation," Bruno said, drawing nods of agreement and laughs from Donati and Donais.

AUTHOR'S NOTES

This is a work of fiction, and the characters within are not meant to depict nor implicate anyone in the actual world. Representations of corruption, illegal activities, and actions taken by governments, corporations, or institution officials were done for the sake of the storyline. They don't represent or imply any illegality or nefarious activity by those who occupy or have occupied positions within them. However, as stated below, substantial portions of *The Collector* are factual.

The United Arab Emirates is a fantastic place to visit, and if you have the opportunity, you should tour the country. The cities are very safe, clean, and unpolluted; the crime rate is extremely low; and the cell reception is so good there doesn't seem to be a dead spot outside the deep desert. If you're up for it, take a camel or horse ride tour through the desert and stay overnight, living like a Bedouin in the comfortable accommodations the tour company arranges.

As written, there are six royal families in the United Arab Emirates. Although Al Nahyan and Al Qasimi are two of the six ruling families, Walid Al Nahyan and Faisal Al Qasimi are fictional characters who don't represent past or present royal family members. Interestingly, when I selected names for the characters in my manuscript and researched those common in various cities, I came across these names. I thought they'd be suitable for the sheiks who facilitated the thefts of masterpieces, not knowing they were associated with the country's ruling families. Needless to say, no one in the UAE's royal families is accused of wrongdoing or improprieties, and you should not associate actual persons with the acts that I've attributed to fictional characters.

The Vatican Museums are a complex of fifty-four museums spread over one thousand four hundred rooms, chapels, and galleries. These contain seventy thousand works of art, twenty thousand of which are displayed in twenty-four galleries or rooms, including the Sistine Chapel. As written, the museum's hierarchy begins with the pope, extends to the secretary general of the Vatican's Governorate, and ends with the curator. There are no trustees, governing boards, or committees. Therefore, the museums have minimal bureaucracy. You can read more on the Vatican's most famous paintings, including Raphael's Transfiguration, at (https://www.walksinrome.com/blog/ raphaels-last-work-the-transfiguration-vatican-museums-rome#:~:text=The%20Transfiguration%3A%20Raphael's%20 Last%20Work&text=However%2C%20the%20painting%20 never%20left,the%20high%20altar%20until%201797.) and (https://theromanguy.com/italy-travel-blog/vatican-city/ vatican-museums/most-famous-paintings-at-the-vatican/).

Most museums show a small percentage of their art, the limitation being a lack of space. The Tate displays twenty percent of its permanent collection, the Louvre exhibits eight percent, the Guggenheim shows three percent, and the Berlinische Galerie puts two percent of its art on display (https://www.bbc.com/culture/ article/20150123-7-masterpieces-you-cant-see). Although there's no way to know with certainty how many forgeries are on display in the average museum, some estimate it to be as high as twenty percent. Other articles I've read set the percentage at between one and fifty percent. As an example, police found that eighty-two of the one hundred forty-two works at the Museé Terrus in Elne, France, were forgeries.

(https://www.nationalgeographic.com/culture/article/fake-art-france-culture-spd). Additionally, some estimate that forty to fifty percent of art being sold as authentic are forgeries or are misattributed (https://www.arnabontempsmuseum.com/how-many-paintings-in-museums-are-forgeries/#:~:text=There%20 is%20a%20significant%20amount,today%20is%20forged%20 or%20misattributed.).

The pope in my novel is fictional and does not represent the current pontiff. For the storyline to work, I needed his birthplace to be the same as Leonardo da Vinci, who was born in the Italian hamlet of Anchiano, a fifty-mile car ride from Florence. No past or present pope was born in this hamlet.

Leonardo was the illegitimate son of a twenty-five-year-old notary, Ser Piero, and a peasant girl, Caterina. Although his father took custody of him after birth, he spent the first five years of his life with his mother in Anchiano before moving in 1457 to the small town of Vinci, which was two miles away, where he lived in the household of his father, grandparents, and uncle.

The Mona Lisa, a portrait of Lisa Gherardini, was commissioned by her husband, a wealthy silk merchant, to celebrate their new home and the birth of their second son. It isn't painted on canvas but on a poplar plank, the medium a common practice for Renaissance artists, and accounts for its weight of nearly eighteen pounds. The Louvre has ten million visitors annually, eighty percent of whom visit the Mona Lisa. The painting is kept in a temperature and humidity-controlled bulletproof glass case behind a barricade, preventing visitors from getting too close. The painting has only left France three times: once in 1963 for display in the United States at the request of Jacqueline Kennedy, and in 1974 to be exhibited in Japan and the Soviet Union. It has never been exhibited in Italy. Interestingly, during Napoleon's rule, the Mona Lisa was hung in his bedroom. You can find additional information on this remarkable masterpiece and the facts used in my manuscript by going to (https://dreamsinparis.com/

facts-about-mona-lisa/) and (https://www.csmonitor.com/From-the-news-wires/2010/0716/Mona-Lisa-examination-reveals-layers-of-paint-for-dreamy-quality#:~:text=Specialists%20 from%20the%20Center%20for,meet%20his%20standards%20 of%20subtlety.). As stated, the iconic painting is removed from its display case each year and inspected by restoration experts. You can learn more about this process at (https://robbreport.com/ shelter/art-collectibles/if-you-win-this-auction-you-can-get-up-close-and-personal-with-the-mona-lisa-1234584212/).

As represented, the Mona Lisa was stolen from the Louvre in 1911 by three Italian handymen—two brothers, Vincenzo and Michele Lancelotti, and the ringleader, Vincenzo Perugia. Louvre officials didn't know the masterpiece was missing until a still-life artist asked an employee when the photographers would bring it down from the roof and return it to its display area, the practice at the time being to photograph paintings in the sunlight where the lighting was superior to anything created indoors. Subsequently, the theft wasn't discovered for twenty-eight hours. You can find more information on the theft of the Mona Lisa at (https://www. npr.org/2011/07/30/138800110/the-theft-that-made-the-mona-lisa-a-masterpiece). The breach of the Louvre's computer system and the indefinite length of time the museum supposedly keeps its security camera footage were inserted for the sake of the story and does not reflect their current or past security practices.

The referenced painting techniques of Leonardo da Vinci are accurate. He typically painted with oil, making his colors from ground pigments. He also made tempera, a fast-drying painting medium consisting of colored pigments mixed with a glutinous water-soluble binder, which was usually egg yolk.

Da Vinci would generally begin a painting by covering the canvas with a pale gray or brown underpainting, atop which he'd layer transparent glaze within a small range of tones, using natural hues that were muted in intensity. As referenced, he used glazes in a technique known as sfumato. Meaning "like smoke," it consisted of applying dark glazes instead of blunt colors to add depth. You can find more on Leonardo's painting techniques, including the information incorporated into my manuscript, by reading the following article by Leon Grey: (https://www.davincilife. com/article4-davinci-painting-technique.html#:~:text=The%20 Leonardo%20da%20Vinci%20painting,neutral%20grays%2C%20 typically%20for%20underpainting.&text=Leonardo%20 incorporated%20glazes%20using%20the%20da%20Vinci%20 painting%20technique%20of%20sfumato.).

The reference to da Vinci using thirty layers of paint to create subtlety, and that the combined layering was less than forty micrometers, half the thickness of a human hair, can be found in a *Christian Science Monitor* article at (https:// www.csmonitor.com/From-the-news-wires/2010/0716/ Mona-Lisa-examination-reveals-layers-of-paint-for-dreamy-quality#:~:text=Specialists%20from%20the%20Center%20 for,meet%20his%20standards%20of%20subtlety.).

The science of detecting art forgeries, which I incorporated into the manuscript, was taken from the following articles: (https://www.portableas.com/news/identifying-fake-art-and-artifacts/), (https://www.futurelearn.com/info/courses/art-crime/0/steps/11884), (https://www.artexpertswebsite.com/ authentication/scientific-tests.php), and (https://artrepreneur. com/journal/authenticating-art/). I used only the XRF detection method at the Vatican Museums because it was fast and allowed me to get on with the story rather than bog the reader down with the inevitable—that the painting was a fake.

An interesting article by Samanth Subramanian in the June 15, 2018 edition of *The* Guardian will give you an insight into how forgeries are made. The article explains the pigments used by the artists, how to analyze the cracks in various paintings based on the period in which they were done, the type of canvas used, and other factors employed to determine the authenticity of a work. You can find this amazing article at (https://www.

theguardian.com/news/2018/jun/15/how-to-spot-a-perfect-fake-the-worlds-top-art-forgery-detective).

Art forgers are prolific, some producing over a thousand fakes that are impossible to discern from the original without scientific verification. One of the more remarkable forgers was Mark Augustus, who impeccably copied artists such as Picasso and, donning different disguises, donated the fakes to museums, which meant he wasn't violating any laws because it's not illegal to replicate a painting if you don't sell it as the original work. Pei-Shen Qian is a master forger famous for copying the post-impressionist paintings of such artists as Matisse and André Derain. One of his forgeries sold for eighty million dollars. Wolfgang Beltracchi is a master forger who replicated approximately thirteen hundred paintings. You can learn more about these master forgers and others in an April 1, 2021 article by Joe Latimer at (https://www.joelatimer.com/7-of-the-most-famous-art-forgers-in-history/).

The Louvre is the largest museum in the world, with over six hundred and fifty-two thousand square feet of exhibition space dedicated to its permanent collection. Originally built as a fortress in 1190, it was reconstructed in the sixteenth century as a palace. Having been repurposed in August 1793, it opened as a museum with a collection of five hundred thirty-seven paintings. Its current collection comprises four hundred eighty thousand works of art, with an estimated value in excess of thirty-five billion dollars. The palace and grounds of the Louvre have an estimated value of ten and a half billion dollars. (https://www.livescience.com/31935-louvre-museum.html) and (https://livtours.com/blog/10-cool-facts-about-the-louvre/#:~:text=According%20to%20French%20historian%20Patrice,years%20to%20accumulate%20this%20wealth.).

In my research, it was difficult to accurately establish the organization and number of staff employed within the restoration and preservation departments of the Louvre. Instead, I described similar areas at the Metropolitan Museum of Art in New York.

Because they're both massive museums, I believed they would be similarly organized and have relatively the same number of conservators, conservation scientists, conservation preparators, restorers, and so forth. The division of the restoration area for paintings into an area that specialized in Renaissance-era art was done for the storyline. You can find information on restoration and preservation efforts at The Met at (https://www.metmuseum.org/about-the-met/conservation-and-scientific-research/conservation-stories/history-of-conservation).

Because the Louvre sits in a flood zone on the right bank of the Seine, a river that frequently floods, the museum's hierarchy decided it needed a plan to protect not only its works on display but also those in its storage facilities—which consist of over sixty locations inside and outside the Louvre (https://www.louvre.fr/en/the-louvre-in-france-and-around-the-world/the-louvre-conservation-centre). Many works, such as marble sculptures, are heavy and difficult to move quickly. Therefore, the Louvre Conservation Center was constructed at a cost of seventy-three million dollars. The 2.4-acre site is in the northern French commune of Liévin and can store two hundred fifty thousand works of art. The facility's protective features include a double-waterproofed roof with unique leak detection technology, green lights that capture harmful bugs such as the common furniture beetle, and security systems programmed to shield artifacts from fire and terrorist attacks. You can read more about this center by going to Jacob Muñoz's February 19, 2021 article in Smithsonian Magazine at (https://www.smithsonianmag.com/smart-news/how-louvre-protecting-its-cultural-treasures-against-extreme-weather-180977063/).

My description of the Louvre's security is fictional. It was conjured to fit my story and provide a way for Montanari to give Bruno, Donati, and Donais a thread that, if they kept pulling, would put them on the trail of the Mona Lisa. Likewise, the method used to penetrate the Louvre's computer system is fictional and was done for the sake of the story because I needed an archival record of what occurred in the restoration area. Therefore, ignore the machinations that Montanari used to penetrate that system which, while it made sense to the author, would likely send a competent programmer to their local bar.

Most are surprised to learn there's a Louvre Abu Dhabi. The cost to license that name and build the museum in the United Arab Emirates didn't come cheap. This ninety-two thousand square feet structure cost one hundred eight million dollars, on top of the five hundred twenty-five million dollars that the city of Abu Dhabi paid the French government to license the name "Louvre" for thirty years and six months. Additionally, this license requires the UAE government to pay an additional seven hundred forty-seven million dollars in fees for borrowing works of art, providing special exhibitions, and curatorial services, whatever that means. The museum is on Saadiyat Island and consists of fifty-five separate small buildings in a vast hall capped by a five-hundred-and-ninety-foot dome constructed with seven thousand tons of steel. It's magnificent. (https://qz.com/1070765/the-louvre-abu-dhabi-will-open-on-november-11-after-decades-of-planning-and-1-4-billion-spent#:~:text=A%20decade%20in%20the%20making,Louvre%E2%80%9D%20name%20for%2030.5%20years.).

The art forgery techniques described in my novel are accurate and taken from a January 16, 2022 article in *ScienceABC* by Sanjukta Mondal.

In my manuscript, I shortened Milani's explanation of how paintings are forged so it wouldn't bog down the storyline. However, if you'd like more detail, the article below goes into various techniques employed by forgers, including using tea or coffee to adjust the tint. I was surprised to read that Michelangelo was a forger at the beginning of his career and, in those endeavors, used smoky fire and tea to tint paper. (https://www.scienceabc.com/eyeopeners/how-exactly-is-a-piece-of-art-faked.html).

The method for mounting and riding a camel is as described and taken from the following articles: (https://www.wikihow.com/Ride-a-Camel) and (https://www.onthegotours.com/blog/2011/02/how-to-ride-a-camel/). Interestingly, camel stirrups aren't used for riding but for getting on and off. Also, for a more comfortable ride, if that's possible, I was surprised to learn that you should cross your legs around the saddle post, distributing your body weight toward the rear and tailbone. This makes for a much more bearable ride because you sway with the camel's natural gait—a tip I could have used to survive my initial camel ride. However, after several enthusiastic treks to try to become proficient at riding, I can tell you with certainty that riding a camel will never be comfortable. In addition to distributing one's weight, the best advice I can give is to pop an over-the-counter pain reliever thirty minutes before your ride.

How world leaders and centers of influence contact one another is accurately described and taken from a February 10, 2006 article by Daniel Engber published by the Slate Group. You can find this by going to (https://slate.com/news-and-politics/2006/02/how-world-leaders-make-phone-calls.html). However, no system is foolproof. The following is from the above article: *This verification process doesn't always work. The article mentions that in 2003 a pair of radio DJs in Miami had a woman with a Cuban accent call Venezuelan President Hugo Chavez claiming she was one of Fidel Castro's operators and that he was at a secret location and couldn't be called back. These DJs received (Chavez's) direct number from a Venezuelan officer to whom they were connected. A few months later, they contacted Castro posing as Chavez.*

The definition of cut-outs was taken from *Spy*, a good reference for those wanting a better understanding of the lexicon of spycraft. You can find this at (https://www.spymuseum.org/education-programs/spy-resources/language-of-espionage/#:~:text=Cut%2Dout,a%20spymaster%20and%20other%20subagents.).

The International Merchant's Bank of Abu Dhabi is fictional, as is King's Heritage Bank. They don't exist. In researching the guidelines for a major bank's lending requirements using art as collateral, I came upon the policy of the Bank of America's Private Bank, which you can view at (https://www.privatebank. bankofamerica.com/articles/your-art-collection-as-loan-collateral.html#:~:text=Not%20every%20collector%20and%20 collection,among%20artists%20and%20time%20periods.). They seem typical of other major banks, at least the ones I researched. They require an internationally recognized collection valued at more than ten million dollars, with a minimum loan amount of five million dollars. The loan is typically fifty percent of the appraisal. Because art fluctuates in value, the bank appraises it annually and adjusts the value accordingly. The bank also likes to see a diversified portfolio consisting of various artists. They believe that artists sometimes suffer softness in the market and that this weakness could significantly devalue the portfolio without diversification. The bank ties its annual interest rate to the Bloomberg Short Term Bank Index daily floating rate plus a spread. My apologies to the BofA if I screwed up any of their terms. The above link provides the attorney-scrutinized details.

Edward Stanley's office is a description of Prince William's home office at Kensington Palace and was taken from the following article, the only exception being that I placed another chair beside the couch rather than a plant. My apologies to the decorator; I needed the seating space.

Kensington Palace was built in 1605. It was the birthplace and childhood home of Queen Victoria and is the current residence of the Prince and Princess of Wales. The four hundred eighty-four thousand square feet palace has five hundred forty-seven rooms. Interestingly, the State Rooms are open to the public and are managed by an independent charity that does not receive public funds. The offices and private accommodation areas are the responsibility of the royal household.

(https://www.hellomagazine.com/homes/20211015124019/ prince-william-home-office-kensington-palace-photo/).

As represented, the British Museum is accused of being the world's largest receiver of stolen goods. In the following November 4, 2019 article in *The Guardian* by Dalya Alberge (https://www.theguardian.com/world/2019/nov/04/british-museum-is-worlds-largest-receiver-of-stolen-goods-says-qc), Alberge reveals that most of this stolen property is not on public display and that the British government refuses to return them to the country of origin. The return of the Elgin marbles, Hoa Hakananai'a, and the Benin bronzes are sought by the governments of Greece, Easter Island, and Nigeria, respectively. Concerning the Elgin marbles, the British base their refusal to return them on a contention that Lord Elgin salvaged and afterward legally obtained the pieces with the approval of the Ottoman authorities at the time. The Rosetta Stone (https://www.pbs.org/newshour/world/egyptians-call-on-british-museum-to-return-the-rosetta-stone) was uncovered by French scientists in 1799 in the northern Egyptian town of Rashid after Napoleon's occupation. When British forces defeated the French in Egypt, it and a dozen other antiquities were handed over to the British under the terms of the 1801 surrender between the opposing army generals. There are further examples of foreign antiquities that went to Britain, but you get the point.

Hushed exists and enables the user to make private calls, send anonymous texts, hide their caller ID with a fake phone number, and manage multiple lines. It uses a Wi-Fi/data connection, negating the need for an actual phone number or SIM card in over three hundred area codes in the United States, Canada, and Great Britain. You can read more about Hushed by going to (https://support.hushed.com/hc/en-us/articles/360015710391-What-is-Hushed-).

I made up the name Philippe Pastor because I thought it would be easy for readers to remember, which was important because my novels tend to have quite a few characters. However, when I researched the name, I discovered that Philippe Pastor is a well-known French artist born in Monaco and has exhibited works worldwide. You can learn more about the artist and his works at (https://www.artsandcollections.com/article/philippe-pastor-artist-of-nature-art/).

Saint-Paul-de-Vence is a medieval town with narrow stone streets and beautiful houses and buildings that provide a magnificent view of the Côte d'Azur. Because I needed Ulrick and Karin's home near the Colombe d'Or Hotel, I modified the area around the Golden Dove to be visible from its terrace. Additionally, I took liberties with my description of the hotel for the sake of the storyline, although I consider the alterations minor. I've been to this charming town several times, most recently to reacquaint myself with its visual appeal so that I could accurately incorporate it into my manuscript. If you want an in-depth description of Saint-Paul-de-Vence, read the December 24, 2020 post: *Steve and Carole in Vence.* (https://steveandcaroleinvence.com/saint-paul-de-vence/).

Saint-Jean-Cap-Ferrat is the second most expensive real estate on the planet, next to a residential property in Monaco. Reinhard Vogel's estate was a modification of the nearly four hundred million dollars former French Riviera residence of Belgian King Leopold II. Known as Villa Les Cèdres, it was built in 1830 and has a footprint of thirty-five acres. The estate was later owned by the Marnier-Lapostolle family of Grand Marnier fame. Italian distiller Davide Campari-Milano SpA acquired the fourteen-bedroom mansion and estate with the sale of Grand Marnier. For the sake of the story, I added the guardhouse and, having never received an invitation to visit Villa Les Cèdres, improvised its interior. It should go without saying the current and past owners of this or other estates in Saint-Jean-Cap-Ferrat, or anywhere else, were not involved in the theft of art or other illegalities represented in this work of fiction. You

can read more about Villa Les Cèdres at (https://thespaces.com/
worlds-most-expensive-home-is-up-for-grabs-for-e350m/).

The information on the looting of art by the Nazis is accurate,
with the obvious exception that Hitler did not select Reinhard
Vogel's father, who is fictional, to pilfer art, antiquities, or
anything else from occupied countries. In researching Hitler's
looting, I found numerous locations where art and other valuables
were hidden during WWII. Interestingly, many stolen valuables
were taken to Switzerland and stored in bank vaults. One Nazi
repository for looted art was Austria's Salzwelten Altaussee salt
mine, which has been in continuous operation since 1147. In
1943 it became a Nazi repository for eight thousand solen works
of art, with most destined for the prospective Führermuseum,
planned for Hitler's hometown of Linz, Austria. The one hundred
thirty-seven tunnels in that mine have a constant temperature
of forty-six degrees Fahrenheit and are twenty-six hundred feet
below the surface, providing an ideal environment for the pilfered
art and protection against allied bombings. Other salt mines used
to store stolen art were the Kaiseroda salt mine complex near
Merkers, situated in the Thüringen region of Germany, and a
mine in Siegen, Germany. Looted art was also kept above ground,
notably at Neuschwanstein Castle in southwest Bavaria and the
Tiergarten Flak Tower in Berlin. You can find articles describing
these locations at (https://www.atlasobscura.com/places/
altaussee-salt-mine#:~:text=During%20World%20War%20
II%2C%20the,and%20private%20collections%20in%20Europe.),
(https://www.thefirstnews.com/article/letter-revealing-last-
known-movements-of-wwiis-most-important-looted-artwork-
uncovered-34293), (https://en.wikipedia.org/wiki/Nazi_
storage_sites_for_art_during_World_War_II), (https://www.
vanityfair.com/news/2014/04/degenerate-art-cornelius-gurlitt-
munich-apartment), and (https://www.archives.gov/publications/
prologue/2002/summer/nazi-looted-art-1).

When researching how to take down a power grid, I read several interesting articles which contrasted sharply with Hollywood versions. In other words, it was far more complicated than portrayed in a movie. I incorporated relevant information from the following articles into my manuscript, taking liberties for the sake of the storyline. You can find these articles at (https://www.utilitydive.com/news/sophisticated-hackers-could-crash-the-us-power-grid-but-money-not-sabotag/603764/), (https://www.wired.com/story/hacking-a-power-grid-in-three-not-so-easy-steps/), and (https://money.cnn.com/2017/07/28/technology/future/crashoverride-black-hat-blackouts-energy-grid/index.html).

Although Edgard Bence is fictional, The Mission for Research and Restitution of Spoliated Cultural Property exists and was created by the French government in 2019 to search for and return paintings, drawings, sculptures, and antiquities looted or sold under duress during World War II. You can read more about this in an April 15, 2019 *New York Times* article by Aurelein Breeden at (https://www.nytimes.com/2019/04/15/arts/design/france-art-looted.html#:~:text=The%20creation%20of%20the%20task,announced%20shortly%20after%20that%20speech.).

ABOUT THE AUTHOR

Alan Refkin has written fourteen previous works of fiction and is the co-author of four business books on China, for which he received Editor's Choice Awards for *The Wild Wild East* and *Piercing the Great Wall of Corporate China*. In addition to the Mauro Bruno detective series, he's written the Matt Moretti-Han Li action-adventure thrillers and the Gunter Wayan private investigator novels. He and his wife Kerry live in southwest Florida, where he's working on his next Mauro Bruno novel.